Silver Dawn

G.J. Walker-Smith

Silver Dawn

Print Edition

© 2014 G.J. Walker-Smith

Cover by Scarlett Rugers, http://www.scarlettrugers.com
Formatting by Polgarus Studio, http://www.polgarusstudio.com

Other Books by G.J Walker-Smith
Saving Wishes (Book One, The Wishes Series)
Second Hearts (Book Two, The Wishes Series)
Sand Jewels (Book 2.5, The Wishes Series)
Storm Shells (Book Three, The Wishes Series)
Secret North (Book Four, The Wishes Series)
Star Promise (Book Five, The Wishes Series)

Contact the author:
https://www.facebook.com/gjwalkersmith
gjwalkersmith@gmail.com
gjwalkersmith.com

To Hannah, a real life, gert lush angel.

CONTENTS

Alex

1. BLACK CROWS

I hate black crows. There's something about their beady eyes and jet black feathers that terrifies me. I'd rather encounter a great white shark while surfing than one black crow in the garden.

I blame Charli.

Even as a little girl she could smell fear. Once she caught on to my aversion to the beastly black birds, she started torturing me with a creepy little poem.

One crow for sorrow,
Two crows for mirth,
Three crows for a wedding,
Four crows for a birth.

She even perfected the horror movie voice and demon expression while reciting it. To this day, I find it hard to fathom how a child of mine could so closely resemble something out of *The Exorcist*.

The poem stuck with me for a few reasons. First, I rarely see more than one crow at a time, which is disturbing. Second, when I do see two together they bring me no happiness. There's no mirth to be had when crows are around.

Gabrielle found the whole notion hilarious.

We stood on the veranda, looking down at the evil crow annihilating the apple tree near the driveway.

"Why does it trouble you so much?" she asked, giggling. "It's just a harmless bird."

I pointed at the tree but looked at her. "It's evil, Gabrielle," I insisted. "It's an apple stealing, evil scavenger."

"They're only apples."

"Today they're apples," I muttered. "What happens when apples don't satisfy him anymore? When he storms the veranda and steals you away, I won't save you."

She rubbed her hand over her big belly. "I'd like to see him try," she replied. "If he can lift me off my feet, he deserves to have me."

My eyes drifted back to the crow and the excess of wasted fruit that was thudding to the ground. An eight-month pregnant French woman might just be his match, especially Gabrielle. She wouldn't exactly go quietly.

"Is it the colour of them that troubles you?" she asked.

"Partly," I muttered, still staring the crow down.

"I might paint some crows." It almost sounded as if she was threatening me. "I shall include them on the mural wall in the nursery."

Gabi had been talking about her mural wall for months, but it had remained blank while she waited for inspiration to hit. As far as I was concerned, black crows were not inspiration. Our kid would never sleep if he had a wall of feathered beasts staring at him.

"That's one of the worst suggestions I've ever heard you make."

She dropped her head and laughed. "I won't make them black. It shall be my interpretation. They'll be blue and orange and fabulous."

I took a step to the side and draped my arm over her shoulder. "They'll still be crows, Gabs."

2. BABY SHOWER

Gabrielle was high maintenance lately, which meant I needed to spend more time at home. Hanging out with her was hardly a chore, but being at the café while Lily Tate was working was.

I'd wrestled with the decision to hire her for weeks before actually biting the bullet and giving her a job. Beggars can't be choosers. A job in a small town café wasn't exactly a sought after position and after a month of advertising, Lily was the only one who applied. That made me a beggar.

"How do you think they get the sugar into these tiny packets?" asked Lily, waving the sachet at me.

I shrugged. "They use tiny people with tiny hands. They're called sugar loaders."

"Oh," she drawled. "Cool job."

I shook my head, marvelling at the idiocy. "Lily, don't you have something to do?"

She straightened up and dropped the sugar packet on the counter. "Yes, actually. I was wondering if I could go home early today. It's Jasmine's baby shower."

I did all I could to stop myself shuddering. Jasmine's baby announcement came just three weeks after ours. The Davis baby was already a superstar around town. Everybody knew about him, and according to Lily, he already had over a hundred Facebook friends. The stupidity was relentless.

"Yeah, you can go," I permitted. "I'm sure Jasmine needs you more than I do."

"She always needs me." She rolled her eyes. "Wade's pretty much useless."

I agreed. Every time he came into the café, conversation would invariably turn to babies. The last little bonding chat we had was particularly difficult.

"I just can't see how she's going to get that thing out," he said making me cringe. "She's going to squeal like a pig."

He was probably right, but I tried not to put too much thought into it. Picturing Jasmine in that light is something I'd never fully recover from.

"You should've heard her scream when the twins were born," he'd added.

The Davis twins were born about a year after Bridget, arriving to fanfare and celebration befitting a royal baby. As far as proud fathers go, Wade was the proudest. He'd taken it as some kind of massive personal achievement.

"Two at once," he marvelled when I congratulated him. "That's some awesome breeding right there."

That was a matter of opinion. The boy, Lincoln, was a little terror. I thought he was shifty from the first minute I laid eyes on him. At the time, Gabrielle had scolded me for saying so.

Once he became mobile and started tearing up the café every time his mother brought him in, she soon changed her tune.

The girl was a little less hardcore. Wade and Jasmine named her Cheyne, but insisted that everyone call her Cheynie.

"We don't want people thinking she's a boy," Wade explained.

There wasn't much chance of that mistake being made. The poor little thing was constantly dolled up in an excess of pink and glitter. Every time I saw her I became just that little bit more thankful to be having a son. I'd done my time with all things pink and sparkly. I was looking forward to dirt and snails.

Gabrielle had never had anything good to say about Jasmine, and now that they had babies due around the same time relations were even more strained. Despite this, she still accepted an invitation to the Davis baby shower.

She arrived at the café just a few minutes after Lily left, looking totally miserable.

"What's wrong, Gabs?"

"I do not want to go to the party, Alex," she announced, frowning.

At least she was being polite about it. My Marseillaise princess had always been a tad dramatic, but nothing compared to the ramped up pregnant version I was dealing with these days. She'd even taken to swearing on occasion, usually out of context, but always with passion.

"Don't go then," I suggested. "You can spend the afternoon with me."

Gabi slowly walked over to the counter, because Gabi walked slowly everywhere. "What do you have planned?"

"I'm going to the cottage to pick up Bridget's cot," I replied. "I think it's time we set it up in the nursery."

"I haven't finished painting the wall yet," she complained.

I reached for her hand and pulled her a step closer to me. "Babe, you haven't started the wall yet," I reminded. "He can do without a mural. He can't do without a bed."

3. TEMPER-MENTAL

Gabrielle was too polite to blow off the baby shower. Our plan was to make a five minute appearance, hand over the gift and bolt. Gabi obviously couldn't run, but I promised to carry her if Wade gave chase.

I opened her door and helped her out of the car. "This is very bizarre, Alex," she grumbled.

I had to agree. Hosting a baby shower at a winery seemed a little odd.

Traipsing around in stiletto heels and a tight fitting leopard print dress while heavily pregnant seemed odd too, but that's the look Jasmine was working as she tottered across the car park with her arms outstretched.

"Ooh, you made it!" she squealed.

Gabi expertly deflected her hug by using her belly as a shield.

Jasmine took a step back and looked Gabrielle up and down. "Geez, you're getting big, aren't you?"

I put a protective arm around Gabi. "You're stretching those spots out quite nicely too, Jasmine," I noted.

The Beautiful looked down at her belly before glaring back at me. "You should go inside, Alex," she said. "Wade will be happy to see you."

I shook my head, trying to look apologetic. "I'm sorry, but we're not staying," I told her. "We just came to give you this."

Wade seemed to appear out of nowhere, just in time to grab the gift as I tried handing it to Jasmine. He held it to his ear and rattled it. "That's very generous of you," he said. "We've cleaned up pretty good as far as gifts go. Much better than the twins' haul – and there were two of them."

Gabrielle let out a little groan. As far as subtly goes, that's as good as it gets for her.

I reached for her hand. "Well, we should be going," I told them.

"Yes," agreed Jasmine, shooting Gabi a look of pity. "Being that big must be awful. You must get so tired."

I opened the passenger door of the car and practically forced Gabi in. "Take your wife back inside, Wade," I urged. "For her own good."

He answered me with a stiff nod, hooked his arm through Jasmine's and led her away. "Let's go, babes," he urged. "You know how temper-mental Gabi can be."

Gabrielle was still ranting when I slipped into the driver's seat. "Temper-mental?" she grumbled. "That is not English. He does not know English."

"Put your seatbelt on, Gabs," I said dully.

"That wasn't English, Alex."

"I know. Put your belt on."

"Temper-mental is not a word."

I pulled her seatbelt across her belly and clicked it into place. "Can we go now, please?" I asked hopefully.

"No, Alex." Gabi folded her arms as best she could. "Go back in there and tell him that temper-mental is not a word."

I leaned across and planted a kiss on her cheek. "I love you. You drive me insane, but I love you."

"Even though I'm fat?" she asked.

I turned the key in the ignition. "Especially because you're fat and temper-mental."

Her wonderful laugh filled the car and I knew that for now, the drama had passed. I understood Gabrielle's epic mood swings perfectly. Being in control was important to her, and none of the changes going on in her body at that point were controllable. That meant she was constantly wound tighter than an eight day clock.

The baby wasn't playing by her carefully set rules, which didn't surprise me in the least. My children are rule breakers, even before they're born.

Her organic diet plan went out the window in the second month when a relentless addiction to instant custard kicked in. Not even Gabi could see any benefit in eating organic vegetables when her main source of sustenance came from a box of custard powder. Her fitness regime fell apart too. Walking further than the letterbox was a major coup lately.

The one plan that did remain was her plans for the big day. I thought the whole notion of a written birth plan was ridiculous, but Gabrielle was insistent.

"No drugs," she declared.

Reasoning with her was impossible, but I tried. "Gabs, you don't know what you're going to want when you're doubled over in pain."

She made a few adjustments to her written birth plan after that. As well as her 'no drugs' rule, 'no pain' was also added to the list.

4. THE LOST BOYS

Spending time at the cottage wasn't something I enjoyed these days.

It was a harsh reminder that Charli, Adam and Bridget were gone. I still expected the little girl with the mop of blonde hair and gumboots to come running at me every time I opened the door.

Six months was too long between visits. Charli had made a vague promise to try and come home for Christmas, but I never pushed the issue. They were settled in New York, and I was happy for them.

I unlocked the door and ushered Gabi in ahead of me. "Can you smell that?" she asked, wandering to the centre of the lounge room.

"No. What?"

She screwed up her pretty face. "Dust. It smells dusty in here."

I laughed. "You can smell dust now?"

"I have all sorts of super powers lately, Alex."

I sidled up to her, slipped my arms around her middle and whispered in her ear. "I haven't seen you leap any buildings in a single bound for a while, Gabs."

"I do it all the time," she replied. "Usually while you're sleeping."

It was almost plausible. Gabrielle had been keeping superhero hours for months, somehow functioning on just a couple of hours sleep a night.

She had no clue why, but I had a theory. Gabrielle had been waiting over five years to meet our son. He was nearly here, and she was excited. And no one sleeps when they're excited.

She wriggled free of my hold. "Where is the crib?"

"Stored in the shed, I think," I replied.

"Maybe we should buy a new one." Gabi frowned. "It might have spiders on it."

I was almost positive there would be spiders on it, but it was a perfectly good cot that could be cleaned. Bridget used it for less than two years. I saw no sense in buying a new one. "Let's go and check it out." I reached for her hand. "If you're not happy with it, we'll buy a new one."

***

We didn't make it as far as the shed. Gabrielle pulled us to a stop at the edge of the veranda. She stood completely still, staring out at the garden.

"What's wrong?" I asked.

"We are not alone," she mumbled after a long pause.

I turned my head, scanned the garden, and saw nothing.

"Mason, Sean and Tyler," she called. "I see you."

She must've really had pregnant lady superpowers. I didn't see a thing until three little heads popped up from their hiding spots in the garden.

"How did you see us?" asked Tyler. "We're commandos."

Intercepting small soldiers in the garden wasn't out of the ordinary these days. When Flynn found his dream girl a few years ago, he gained an instant family. Hannah was a midwife from Hobart. She moved to the Cove after they married, bringing her raucous boys with her.

Charli jokingly referred to them as the Lost Boys. They were mischievous and borderline naughty, but no match for my kid. Charli's ability to shut them down at every turn impressed them no end.

"You need more training, fellas," I told them.

The boys abandoned their positions and made their way over to us. "We'll have it right before Charli gets back," boasted Tyler. "Are they coming back soon?"

I shook my head, telling him no. The kid tried hard to shrug off the disappointment, but it was obvious. The crush he harboured for Charli was pretty hardcore for a ten-year-old. He'd even told Adam of his plans to steal her away.

"You'd bring her back in a week," replied Adam. "She's hard work."

Tyler wasn't perturbed in the slightest.

His younger brothers weren't quite as extreme, but I was still glad we didn't live at the cottage. Seeing them a couple of times a week was more than enough.

"We have weapons," announced Sean, waving a slingshot at me.

"Were you planning to shoot me?" asked Gabrielle, aghast.

I wrestled the slingshot from Sean's grasp and took a better look at it. "It probably wouldn't do much damage anyway." I pulled the rubber band taut. "The strap is too long."

"No it's not," insisted Tyler, pushing past his brother to get closer to me. "We got Wade a beauty in the arse with a gumnut at close range."

Gabi gasped and immediately scolded him for his choice of words.

Too impressed to feign outrage, I laughed. "Shorten that strap and you'll increase your range," I suggested, handing it back to the boy.

"You're a legend, Alex," declared Tyler. "Can we fix it here?" He pointed to the shed.

"Not a chance."

Sean piped up. "There are awesome tools in there."

I cocked an eyebrow and folded my arms. "And how would you know that?"

"Adam worked in there all the time," he replied casually. "On big boats and stuff."

Gabi alternated her pointed finger between all three boys. "You mustn't ever go in there," she warned.

"We can't get in," volunteered Mason, the littlest brother. "The door is locked."

Sean elbowed him in the side, which backfired on him in an instant. Mason yelled out to their mother and Hannah appeared on the veranda next door a moment later.

Perhaps knowing they were up to no good, she ventured over, scolding each of them with a harsh glare along the way. None of the boys questioned her when she ordered them to go home, which made for an awesome show of authority. They skulked back to their yard in total silence.

"I'm sorry," she said still walking toward us. "They know better than to play over here."

"They're no trouble," insisted Gabrielle sweetly.

Only because we don't live here, I silently added.

Hannah stepped up on to the veranda. "How are you Gabrielle?"

Gabi put her hand to her belly. "Fine. I only have a few weeks to go."

Hannah Davis had the perfect disposition for a nurse. She was always cheerful and happy, except when reprimanding her small soldiers.

Gabi was convinced that her job was the reason for her good nature. "How could she not be happy?" she once asked me. "She sees babies being born every single day."

Gabrielle was desperately hopeful that she'd be on duty for our baby's birth, and made a point of telling Hannah every time she saw her.

"I'm rostered on every other day," she replied. "I'm sure I'll be there at some point."

When chat turned to Gabrielle's ambitious written birth plan, I excused myself and headed to the shed to find the cot. I knew her no-drug-no-pain plan back to front, and it still made no sense to me.

***

It was almost a relief to see that the lock on the shed door was still intact. The Lost Boys might've had a crack at getting in, but Adam had it well secured.

It took a long time to find the crib and all its fixings. It wasn't exactly hidden, but I was distracted by the contents of Boy Wonder's man cave.

It was hard not to feel sorry for Adam. I knew he wasn't keen on the idea of returning to New York, but Charli had wanted to go. And once he finally got his act together, his pledge to give his girls whatever they wanted was a promise he never broke.

I thought he was playing it smart. There was no way Charli would stick it out forever. Life on the beach would eventually beckon again and Adam knew it, which explained why the contents of the shed had been locked up instead of sold off.

"How many spiders have you found?" asked Gabi, poking her head around the doorway.

I turned back to face her. "None. It's perfect, except for the little teeth marks on the edges."

"Bridget ate the cot?" she asked.

I carried the white framework over to her. "I'll touch it up. No big deal."

She ran her fingers over the chipped paintwork. "You're determined to use this crib, aren't you?"

"I like tradition. This is an heirloom cot now," I explained. "Maybe our great grandkids will use it too." I shuddered at the thought. Chances are, we'd still be around to see it. At this rate, I could be a great-grandfather before the age of sixty.

"You're an old soul, Alex," she declared, smiling.

I leaned down and kissed her as I passed. "But I'm a young body, Gabs," I replied. "It's kind of awesome if you think about it."

Gabi caught up to me as I was loading the cot into the back of the car. If she'd hadn't been there, I would've been swearing. I'd surrendered my beloved Ute a few weeks earlier. I was now driving a family friendly SUV. Unlike the Ute it wasn't cot friendly. Having to lower the back seats to fit it in pissed me off. That meant it wasn't Alex friendly either.

Gabi's voice pulled me out of my silent rant. "You're a patriarch, Alex." Her thick French accent made it sound like a seriously hardcore title. "The head of a family. How do you feel about that?"

Before that moment, I'd never given it a thought. "I'm not sure."

"Everything started with you," she continued. "We'd have no need for an heirloom crib if not for you."

I slammed the rear door shut and turned to face her. "That's how we measure the world, Gabs."

I knew I'd lost her when she frowned. "Explain it to me, please."

I reached out and smoothed my hands across her belly, stretching out the white fabric of her dress. "We measure the world by what we leave behind," I explained. "When I'm done, my world will be huge."

5. THE NAME GAME

Putting the cot together took longer than expected. I suspect it had something to do with Gabrielle's micromanagement. "How do you know the screw goes there?" she quizzed.

I looked down at the bolt in question. "Because there's a hole there, babe," I said dryly. "A screw size hole."

She nodded. "You're very handy. I like that about you."

I laughed. "Thank you. You're very arty. I like that about you."

My comment reminded her of the blank wall she was yet to work her magic on. She turned to look at it. "I think I'm going to make a start on the mural soon."

I dropped the screwdriver back in the box and reached for a smaller one. "You've come up with some ideas?"

"Yes," she replied. "A landscape, I think. Perhaps a sunset. That would be serene and calming."

I twisted the tool into the head of the screw. "Sunsets are overrated. Sunrises are where the action is."

I didn't need to look up to know she was staring at me. I could feel the curiosity wafting off her. "Tell me why," she ordered.

"I can't tell you," I teased. "I'd have to show you."

"When?"

"Tomorrow. You come to the beach with me at dawn and I'll show you."

It took Gabi a long time to ponder my offer. I'd tightened every single screw before she replied. "Will you carry me if I get stuck?"

I smiled across at her. "No, I'll just build us a house on the beach," I teased. "When junior's old enough, we'll send him to get help."

"Please do not call him junior," she grumbled. "We must find him a nice name."

The name debate had been ongoing for a while. I favoured classic, simple names that weren't likely to get him beaten up. Gabrielle had a thing for classic names too. The problem was, they were so old-fashioned that none of them had been used since the early 1800s.

"I think we should name him after Renoir, the artist," she suggested.

I could feel myself cringing before she even got the words out. She wasn't surprised by the reaction. It happened a lot when discussing names.

"He was an impressionist," she continued. "His paintings were lovely and bright and vibrant. Renoir didn't use detail to capture detail. He used bold colours."

I stepped over the toolbox and pulled her into my arms. "I love that you're putting so much thought into it." I lightly kissed her lips. "But no son of mine is going to be called Renoir."

She put her hands to my cheeks. "Not Renoir, silly man," she corrected. "His given name was Pierre-Auguste."

"Gabs, Pierre-Auguste would get thumped in the playground just as hard as Renoir."

"Will you at least think about it?"

"No."

She dropped her hold on me in an instant. "There is no reasoning with you."

"I'm a very reasonable man," I insisted. "To prove it, I'm prepared to move the cot to wherever you want it."

Gabi studied the room carefully. "I like it where it is."

I drew her in close again. "See? We're completely in sync. Our son is going to be the most calm and well adjusted child on the planet."

"Pierre-Auguste will be both of those things." She reached up, linking her hands around my neck. "He will be perfect."

6. SILVER DAWN

In June, the sun rises across the Cove a little after 7.30AM.

That meant the hyped up temper-mental French princess was jumping the gun when she dragged me down to the beach at six.

Being early didn't bother me. I could live at the beach indefinitely, but it was cold and dark and no place for Gabs. I managed to stall her by sitting in the car and refusing to move.

No woman on earth looked prettier than Gabrielle when she was pouty and cross, which was fortunate because that was her usual demeanour of late. "If you won't come, I shall go by myself," she threatened.

I leaned across and pushed her door open. "Watch your step, babe," I said casually. "It's dark out there."

A frigid gust of wind swept through the car and she promptly pulled the door closed. "I've changed my mind," she huffed.

"I thought you might," I replied, tilting my head to look up through the windscreen. "It's really black out there."

It was actually the perfect morning to showcase a silver dawn. The heavy cloud cover was exactly what I was hoping for.

"You mustn't confuse blackness with darkness, Alex."

I slipped my arm behind her and tangled my fingers through her hair. "Explain the difference to me."

She held out her hand, palm up. "Well, if I had a palette of red paint, and I mixed black paint with it, the red colour would become cloudy and dull."

"It would," I agreed.

"Darkness doesn't do that," she replied smiling. "If I had a red ruby and I added darkness to it, the ruby would stay beautiful and clear. The red colour would get darker, but never cloudy and dull."

"You're brilliant," I fervently declared. "Beautiful and artistic and brilliant. Teach my son all that you know."

Her lovely soft laugh drifted toward me. "Dark refers to the absence of light, while black is our perception of that absence," she added.

"I love you, Gabrielle," I announced. "I love your French brain and your French heart and your French body." I leaned over and kissed her French lips. "I love everything about you."

Truer words had never been spoken. I'd never met anyone like Gabrielle Décarie. She was smart and feisty and beautiful. She was also guarded, complex and stubborn, which meant she was seriously misunderstood by most. I read her perfectly, and for that reason alone, we were meant for each other.

"Do you know what I love?" she whispered.

"Custard?"

She giggled again. "Yes. I love you and I love custard."

"Which do you love more?" I leaned back and stared at her, making the question seem deadly serious.

Gabi pretended to put some serious thought into her reply. "I'd say you, but that's probably because I don't have any custard right now."

I reached into the back and grabbed a plastic container off the back seat. "I planned ahead and made you some while you were in the shower," I explained.

Her bright green eyes lit up as she took it from my grasp. "You did?"

I handed her a spoon. "I figured it was the least I could do considering you let me knock you up."

"I love you, Alex Blake – even more than custard."

I probably would've believed her if she hadn't been fumbling with the lid of the container like an addict desperate for her next hit. "Put the spoon down and tell me that."

After careful deliberation, Gabi rose to the challenge and set the spoon down on the dashboard. "I love you, Alex Blake. You make wonderful custard."

***

Unlike my Marseillaise princess, I am not complex. I like things to be simple and calm, and nothing could be calmer than sitting in a car at dawn watching the sun lift over the ocean.

Thanks to the high vantage point of the car park, talking Gabrielle out of venturing down to the beach wasn't difficult. Now that she had a belly full of custard *and* baby, hiking probably wasn't an option anyway.

"Why is it called a silver dawn?" she asked, staring out to sea. "I think it's more grey than silver."

"It's definitely silver," I insisted. "Has been for a long time."

She turned, angling her body toward me as best she could. "What makes it silver?"

"If I tell you, you have to promise not to interrupt me." It was a big ask but she nodded as if she could do it. "It was started by a bloke called Rubin," I began. "He had six daughters, and as luck would have it, they were all fairies."

"Six?" she gasped. I looked across at her, silently reminding her of her pledge to keep quiet, which was pointless. She kept talking. "How would one keep track of six fairies?"

I smiled. "I don't know, Gabs. I had enough trouble keeping track of one."

Gabi laughed. "Yes, but you managed."

"Rubin had his work cut out for him too." I reached for her hand. "His youngest daughter, Kia, had a few problems. She was a special needs fairy. Her wings were incomplete," I continued. "They had holes in them so she couldn't fly like her sisters. She could only get as high as the clouds, and then she'd drop back to the ground."

A tale doesn't get much sadder than a grounded fairy. I quickly got to the point so Gabi wouldn't take it to heart and start blubbering. Burning toast was enough to set the waterworks off these days. Unbelievably, she didn't interrupt as I explained Rubin's grand efforts at helping Kia fly.

"He was a silversmith. Every morning he'd patch up the holes in her wings with silver," I explained. "It worked a treat, but only short term. The patches would wear off after a few hours and she'd be grounded again. Rubin would work on her wings all night long just so Kia could spend some time in the air with her sisters every day."

"Artists always show dedication to their craft," boasted Gabi. "It shows true artistry."

I glanced across at her and smiled. "Well, it wasn't always appreciated. Kia was a bit of a handful, always wanting to fly further and longer. Rubin warned her time and time again that if the silver patches wore away while she was flying, she'd crash."

"It angered her?"

"Frustrated the glitter out of her," I replied making her laugh. "So much so that early one morning, Kia made a break for it. She crept out of the house while her family were sleeping and took off for a long dawn flight."

Gabrielle turned her head, focusing back on the silver edged clouds. "I suspect this is where the story takes a turn for the worst."

"She never came home again," I said, inciting a pretty pout. "Presumably her wings failed and she crashed to the ground. Her father spent the next few years crafting a massive blanket out of silver. Now he travels the earth, following daybreaks. Just on sunrise, he fans the blanket out, covering as much of the sky as he can."

"And then?"

I looked out at the rising sun. "He waits and he waits, hopeful that he's finally covering the place where she landed. There's supposedly enough silver in the sky to get Kia airborne again. It's her ticket home."

"I hope he finds her," she said quietly.

"Charli doesn't believe she's lost," I replied. "She thinks she found a way to patch her own wings and is out there exploring the world."

Gabi glanced across at me and smiled. "That would make for a much nicer tale, Alex. Why are all your stories so sad?"

I wasn't entirely sure. It could've had something to do with the fact that most of them had come to me in times of strife. Pulling Charli into line was much easier if the tales I told were of the cautionary variety.

"Fairies aren't always good," I replied. "Some bad eggs run with that crowd."

"They're your stories," she reminded. "You could turn them around and make them see the error of their ways."

I brought her hand to my mouth and kissed her fingers. "They're not my stories, Gabs. Most of them belong to Charli, and Bridget has taken ownership of the others."

7. PURPLE TURTLES

I was hopeful that the last few weeks of Gabrielle's pregnancy would wind down slowly. Gabi had other ideas. She was busier than ever, making sure that every last thing was perfect for the new baby.

She'd been working on her mural wall for days, usually at night because she couldn't sleep. I hadn't been into the baby's room since she began, promising to steer clear until it was time for the big reveal.

As expected, it was worth the wait. When she finally let me in to look at it, every compliment I'd planned to rain on her escaped me.

The landscape painting was intricate and textured, creating so much depth that it was almost as vivid as looking out a window.

I just wasn't sure which planet the window would've been on. The coastal scenery was realistic and familiar. The little animals hiding in the bushes were not. Gabrielle had put her own stamp on them, and it wasn't her usual classic style.

The first thing I noticed was a purple turtle chilling out underneath a perfectly normal green tree. Maybe he was a hippy turtle – he had a pink flower painted on his shell.

"Do you like it?" she asked. "I want you to like it."

I snaked my arms around her hips and stepped closer to her. "I love it, Gabs," I replied truthfully.

"Even the crows?"

I glimpsed at her only briefly. My focus was on finding the ghastly birds in the picture. It took a while because they weren't regular crows. They were blue and orange, just as she'd threatened they'd be.

"I don't like the crows," I muttered.

"Do they look frightening?"

"No," I conceded. They just looked stupid – like Wade Davis with feathers.

Gabrielle stepped in front of me. Her emerald eyes studied me closely. "The things that scare us are never as daunting if you change the way you look at them."

I pulled her in as close as I could without squashing her belly.

"You cannot be afraid of blue crows, Alex," she added. "That would be nonsensical."

Blue crows were nonsensical to begin with, but I was never going to win the argument, and knew better than to try. "It's a nice theory, Gabs," I said diplomatically.

"It's proven fact." She twisted in my arms. "I don't like turtles. See the turtle in my picture? I made him purple. He's not nearly as frightening when he's purple."

I studied the painting closely. She was right. There was nothing frightening about the purple turtle hanging out in the reeds near the beach, but I struggled to imagine him looking sinister in his natural brownish-grey state either.

"What do you have against turtles?"

"They're slow and creep around like villains." She scrunched up her pretty face. "I do not like them, Alex."

I smiled at her. "Unless they're purple."

"Exactly." Her perfect giggle was soft and demure. "Perfectly harmless when purple."

Only Gabrielle could find inspiration in the things that creep us out. If she'd told me her plan of memorialising them on a wall in our son's room I would've vetoed it in an instant.

My lack of vision is just one of the many reasons why I'd make a terrible artist. But Gabrielle, much like my daughter, had a knack for looking at the deeper picture.

8. WINNING

Our son had terrible timekeeping skills. He was two days overdue and wasn't showing any signs of making an appearance. And I suspected his mother was close to losing her mind because of it.

The first hint came when she decided to sew curtains for the baby's room.

Gabi was artistic and creative, but she was no mathematician. She'd somehow calculated that she'd need fifty metres of fabric to do it.

I nearly choked when I saw the massive bolt of striped fabric lying across the back seat of the car.

"How did you lift this?" I asked, throwing it over my shoulder.

"I didn't," she replied. "The saleslady did."

"I hope you paid her extra, Gabs."

"It will not go to waste," she declared, trailing behind me as we walked to the house. "I shall use the rest to accessorise."

I expected that meant cushions or something similar. The reality was a little different. I arrived home from work the next afternoon to an overload of red and white stripes.

"What do you think?" asked Gabi, meeting me at the door.

I slipped my arm around her and took a long look around. "Ah, it looks great."

That was a lie. It looked like a circus tent. Red and white striped lounge room curtains were never going to be a good look.

Gabi grabbed my hand and slowly led me toward the kitchen. "Come and see the rest," she ordered.

"There's more?"

"Yes, I found a use for all of it."

She wasn't kidding. The kitchen looked worse. Not only were the curtains striped, the tablecloth was too.

"You've been busy, Gabs."

"I have," she beamed proudly. "It took me all day."

I leaned down and kissed her. It was the most encouragement I could offer. All I could hope was that once the baby arrived, I'd get my classy, design-savvy Marseillaise princess back and she'd do away with the hideous décor.

***

The craziness continued the next day.

Gabrielle called me at the café to let me know she was heading to Sorell for a day of shopping. I felt a little more comfortable with the idea once she told me she was taking Floss for company – right up until she mentioned that Jasmine was going too.

"You can't stand Jasmine," I reminded.

"But I like shopping, Alex," she protested.

I was too flummoxed to argue with her. I made her promise to call me when she got there and told her to take it easy.

"Of course I will," she replied. "I move slowly."

***

Gabi's idea of taking it easy differed from mine. When I walked through the door that afternoon, I could tell she'd been busy again.

The red and white striped table was perfectly set and I could smell something amazing cooking. How she'd managed that as well as a day of shopping was inconceivable. The only thing more mind-blowing was her appearance.

Gabrielle was beautiful. She had incredible elegance and grace, even when nine months pregnant. The woman standing at the stove looked a little…. different.

The bright pink stretchy dress she wore was horrid. It was short and tight and cheap. It made me wonder where Gabi had gone. And then I wondered if the pregnant streetwalker at the stove knew how to cook.

After a long moment of deliberation, I decided not to question it. I walked over and wrapped my arms around her from behind.

"I didn't hear you come in," she said, twisting to look at me.

I kissed her gently and she kissed me back – Gabi-style, not cheap hooker-style.

"I was trying to be quiet," I teased. "In case you were sleeping."

"I don't sleep."

I kissed her again. "I know."

***

Dinner wasn't the quiet and romantic affair it usually was when Gabi added candles to the table setting. She talked a mile a minute, non-stop, mainly about her adventurous day shopping with Floss and the chief Beautiful.

I barely got a word in, which was fine. The coq au vin was Gabi-style too, which meant I was happy to stay quiet and eat.

"Jasmine took us to this big store." She animatedly threw her arms wide. "They sell everything, Alex. Floss got some new shoes. They cost fifteen dollars." She sounded totally bewildered by the notion, and I knew why.

Décaries grow up differently to most people. They're privileged and advantaged, and generally pretty sheltered because of it. As a result, bargain basement department stores were a mystery to Gabrielle.

"Fifteen dollars?" I asked, trying my hand at sounding impressed.

"Yes," she crowed. "For both of them!"

I tried masking my laugh by speaking again. "I'm glad you had fun."

Gabi set her fork down on her plate leaned back in the chair. "We walked a long way. I was sure baby was going to come." She patted her belly. "But he didn't. He's not going anywhere."

I reached across and splayed my hand across her belly. "He'll come when he's ready," I told her.

"He can stay a while longer," she replied. "I don't feel fat today."

I withdrew my hand and straightened up, studying her errant grin. Replying to a comment like that took serious preparation. The look on her face made it even scarier territory.

Mercifully, she cut me some slack by explaining. "Jasmine taunted me all day with stupid fat jibes. I wanted to whack her, Alex."

I frowned, more than a little annoyed. Jasmine took digs at Gabi the same way she'd tormented Charli over the years – slyly and subtly. It was unoriginal, tiresome and completely unwarranted considering they were both heavily pregnant. "Just ignore her, Gabs. She'll come unstuck eventually."

Her pretty grin broadened. "She did come unstuck. It was fabulous."

I didn't interrupt as she told me the tale. There wasn't any need for encouraging interjections. Gabrielle had finally had a win.

The big store that sold fifteen-dollar shoes also had a clothes section. Jasmine took a liking to an ugly cheap pink dress and took off to the fitting room to try it on.

"I went with her," announced Gabi, sounding like a female Inspector Clouseau. "It didn't fit her. She was nearly crying when she came out."

"Did you put your arm around her a give her a cuddle to cheer her up?" I asked wryly.

"Definitely not." Her wicked laugh made me smile. "It was a size twelve. I wanted to whack her for being so delusional."

"You had a lot of whacking urges today, Gabs," I noted. "I'm glad you held back."

"I gave her a metaphorical whack," she replied. "I snatched the dress from her and went and tried it on myself." Gabi slid her chair back and levered herself to her feet. "It fit me, Alex. I stretched it to the point of splitting, but it fit me." She waved her hands around, showcasing her trashy frock. "I kept it on for the rest of the day, just to prove that I am the queen."

I couldn't keep my hands off her any longer. I pushed my chair back, reached across and pulled her into my lap. "Definitely the queen," I murmured kissing her neck.

"It was the best moment of my life," she said boldly.

I laughed at the absurdity. "The best moment?"

Gabi linked her hand around my neck and took a moment to think things through. "Well, perhaps not the best. The custard tart I had for afternoon tea was the best. It was wonderful."

***

The ugly dress didn't last much longer than dinner. Gabi retreated to the bedroom to change into something more comfortable and less trashy, and I stole a few minutes in the shed.

I hadn't been in there for a while. The ocean had been off limits in the last few days and the sight of my boards tormented me.

Being in the water was akin to being on another planet. Gabi had no way of contacting me while I was out there so for now, surfing was off the agenda.

As soon as I switched the light on at the doorway I noticed that Gabrielle's interior design makeover extended further than the house. The window of my manly, dirty, spider-riddled shed was now sporting red and white striped curtains.

I couldn't even begin to imagine how she'd managed to hang them on her own. Then I realised I probably didn't want to know. I pulled the door closed and headed back to the house.

Gabi met me at the door, looking much more like herself with the exception of my oversized coat draped around her shoulders. "I was coming out to get you," she said.

I took the coat off her and hung it back on the hook. "I was only gone a minute."

"I need that coat," she replied.

I frowned at her. "Are you going somewhere, Gabs?"

"We both are," she calmly explained. "I think my waters have just broken."

I took a quick moment to study her pretty face. I'd seen a million expressions from her in the past few months, but this one was new – a lovely mix of panic and excitement. I took her face in my hands and softly kissed her lips. "We're having a baby tonight, Gabs," I whispered. "Are you ready?"

My hands moved with her as she nodded. "Yes," she confirmed, sounding totally unsure. "I think so."

9. BEST LAID PLANS

Expecting the baby to arrive that night was ambitious. Not much happened throughout the night, and by dawn Gabi's contractions were still a long way apart.

The labour ward looked like a hotel room. The only reminder that it was a hospital came from the odd pieces of equipment that looked out of place against the fancy décor.

I got the impression our time spent in there wasn't going to be as relaxing as a hotel stay. Agitation set in early. Calming myself down was impossible, but I tried to play it down by pacing back and forth to the window.

"What can you see, Alex?" asked Gabi.

The view of the car park was nothing special but the horizon beyond it was spectacular.

"The sun is coming up." I turned back to face her. "It's really special."

The sunrise wasn't the only lovely thing in sight. Gabrielle lay on the bed, propped up by too many pillows. She looked so beautiful, and calmer than I'd seen her in months.

"A silver dawn?" she asked.

I turned my attention back to the outside view. The dark clouds were shifting, allowing the bright sun to bleed through the cracks. The blackened winter clouds melded with the bright sun, creating the perfect mix of silver. It was a brilliant example of a silver dawn.

"It is silver. Do you want to see it?" I made my way back over to the bed. "I'll help you to the window."

She shook her head, and settled further back in the pillows. "No. I'm too tired. I want to rest before the pain starts again."

Her level of fatigue troubled me. The girl who'd been moving a mile a minute for months was finally slowing down, on the worst possible day.

I swept my hand through her hair. "Are you okay?" I asked gently. "You have a long way to go today."

Her smile was slight but lit her whole face. "I'm fine. I don't want you to worry about a thing."

I thought I'd been playing it cool. Gabrielle wasn't supposed to know that I was anxious. I wanted her to think I was collected and perfectly in control.

"I'm not worried," I lied. "I'm just excited."

She blinked a few times as if she was having trouble staying awake. I encouraged her to sleep. Meeting our baby was probably still hours away. A few hours sleep seemed like a good idea.

"I don't want to sleep," she protested, closing her eyes again. "I want you to talk to me."

I pulled the chair closer to the bed and sat down beside her. "What do you want to talk about?"

"Tell me you love me," she mumbled.

I brought her hand to my lips and kissed her fingers. "I do, you know," I confirmed. "More than I'll ever be able to explain."

"I love you, Alex," she whispered. "More than art and books."

Her declaration made me laugh. There was no greater achievement than being loved more than art and books.

I kissed her hand again. "I love you more than the ocean," I countered.

She turned her head, laying her cheek on the pillow, opening her bright green eyes to look at me. "Then I had everything."

"Have, Gabs," I corrected. "I'm not going anywhere."

Her English diction sometimes wavered when she was tired or angry. I usually didn't correct her, but it unsettled me so much that I couldn't let it pass.

Gabrielle smiled, either unruffled by the correction, or too tired to argue with me. "Tell me about the silver dawn. What does it look like?"

I glanced in the direction of the window. "I can't see it from here."

She pulled her hand away, breaking my hold on her. "Go to the window and tell me," she instructed. "Please. I want to know."

I did as she asked because I would've done anything for her. It had been that way for a very long time. I took a long look out the window before speaking, trying to think of how to adequately describe it. "The clouds are heavy," I began. "But the sun is winning. It's getting brighter every second, like a big silver blanket in the sky."

"It sounds lovely."

I turned at the sound of her voice, mainly because it sounded tiny and so far away. "It truly is."

"Keep talking, Alex," said Gabi weakly. "Tell me more."

There really wasn't any new information to give her but I turned back to the window and tried. "Our baby's first sunrise will be your first too."

"You've shown me sunrises before."

"But not as a mother, Gabs," I told her. "You'll be in virgin territory tomorrow."

She didn't answer me so I turned back to see if she was sleeping. I could tell just by looking at her that things weren't right. Her head had dropped to her shoulder and her eyes were closed.

In the blink of an eye something had gone horribly wrong. I don't remember walking back to the bed but I somehow got there. I laid my hand over Gabi's but couldn't feel her touch me back.

She wasn't sleeping. She was gone.

The constant thrumming that rang out in the corridor as I smashed my thumb down on the buzzer wasn't enough. My yell for help was much louder.

Hannah appeared first. Her cheery smile that she'd greeted us with earlier was gone. She was all business now as she moved to the head of the bed and thumped her hand down on the emergency bell.

Within seconds, people flooded the room and for the first time in my life I heard the word 'crashed' used to describe a person's condition. I stepped further and further back from the bed, but couldn't get far enough away from what I was seeing.

Someone lowered the bed to a flat position. A doctor moved to Gabi's side and began CPR. He didn't look panicked. He looked perfectly calm as he rhythmically moved, compressing her chest over and over again. "Perimortum delivery pack, please," he ordered, still remarkably calmly. "Right now."

I had no idea what that was, but it sounded dismal. It was then that my terror amplified to a level I could no longer cope with. My heart was thumping through my chest, driven by pure fear because Gabi's had stopped. I'm sure it wasn't the loudest noise in the room, but all I could hear was the sound of the bag-valve being depressed as they forced breath into her. "Help her." My weak demand came out caught in a choked sob. "Please."

No one seemed to hear me, probably because every single person in the room was doing their level best to do exactly that.

I took one more step backward, slamming my back against the wall next to the window. I turned my head, taking one last glance out at the silver dawn. The sun was still rising, gaining strength and light.

I looked back to the woman I loved, artificially moving as they relentlessly pressed down on her chest. Her light and strength had gone, taking my life with it.

10. MAKING DEALS

Whoever said that we're never sent more than we can handle is a liar. I couldn't handle the horror I'd been burdened with that morning.

The decision to take the baby was made instantly. As I was being bustled out of the room, doctors were preparing to take my son from his mother, right there in the ward.

"Not here," I futilely demanded. "Please, not here."

I would never cope with that.

A nurse moved me toward the door with a firm hand on my back. "There's no time to move her," she inadequately explained. "You can wait outside."

I stood in the corridor near the closed door, trying desperately hard not to think about what was happening on the other side. A hundred silent prayers were made over the next few minutes. I found myself making deals with God for the first time in my life. All I wanted was Gabrielle back. I would've given anything up for that.

A draught of wind hit me as the door violently swung open. A nurse flew out and barrelled down the corridor. She was out of sight before the first word made it out of my mouth so I gave up trying to speak.

The only thing stronger than the need for information was the urge to get away. I walked a few metres further down the hall, buying myself a little distance. It brought no relief. Nowhere was far enough away from that room.

My legs locked at the knees, holding me upright against the wall. I don't know how long I stood there. It may have been minutes, but it felt like hours.

My mind seemed to shut down, and only jolted back into gear when the same nurse that rushed out of the room shot past me again.

The crib she was pushing looked like a little plastic box on wheels.

She said nothing as she passed, and I was too scared to ask her anything.

It was just after seven-thirty in the morning. Everything had gone to hell in a few short hours.

Hannah finally stepped out of the room. I desperately wanted her to smile and tell me everything was fine, but it didn't happen. "I'm sorry, Alex," she said quietly. "Sometimes things don't go to plan."

That was an understatement. Gabrielle was the ultimate planner. I knew her birth plan by heart thanks to the hundreds of hours I'd spent listening to her going over it. Every last detail of how she wanted this day to go had been memorialised on paper.

The universe obviously didn't get the memo.

"Don't tell me sorry, Hannah," I muttered. "Just tell me they're okay. That's all I need to hear right now."

She reached out and gave my arm a supportive squeeze. "We're doing all we can."

I could feel tears welling as anger set in. "How long does it take to do all you can?" I didn't realise I'd raised my voice until she shushed me. Even then, I didn't care. "Why is this happening?"

"Gabrielle went into cardiac arrest," she gently explained.

"She's thirty-three," I growled through gritted teeth. "Healthy thirty-three year-old women don't suddenly go into cardiac arrest."

"She's bleeding, Alex." Her tone was still quiet and calm, but I was furiously shaking my head as if she'd said something foolish.

"No she's not."

"Sometimes it's not always detected early enough," she replied. "The abruption can be internal."

I felt my shoulders slump. I wasn't going to be able to rant and rave my way out of the abysmal situation so for Hannah's sake, I didn't try. "And the baby?"

She touched my arm again. "He was born a few minutes ago. He's fine. You can see him shortly."

Utter relief surged through me at the news, but for some reason I couldn't react.

Hannah gave me a tiny smile but I didn't even come close to smiling in return. I managed a small nod. "I just want to see Gabs."

Her mouth opened as if she was about to speak, but was interrupted when the door flew open again. Hannah grabbed my arm and pulled me aside to make way for the swarm of people hurrying past. The only reason I knew Gabi was on the gurney they were pushing was because I caught a glimpse of her hair.

I stood watching as they disappeared around the corner, praying to God that that wouldn't be my last memory of her.

"They're still trying to stabilise her," explained Hannah. "They're taking her to surgery."

I'm no doctor, but I'm not an idiot either. They weren't winning the battle. She just didn't want to tell me.

I turned back to Hannah. "I want to see my son."

She nodded, motioning toward the door with an upward nod. "Come with me."

***

The room was deathly quiet, which added to the unbearable oppressiveness. I glanced over at the bed as I followed Hannah into the room, noticing it had been completely stripped - almost as if Gabrielle had never been there. It made me feel so ill that I came close to throwing up.

"This way, Alex," she coaxed, leading me toward the small plastic crib.

For the briefest of moments, the universe cut me some slack and allowed me to marvel at the wonder of new life. My tiny son looked perfectly peaceful, despite his traumatic entrance into the world. A little fearful of touching him, I gripped the edge of the crib with both hands as I gazed down at him. He was much bigger than I remembered Charli being. His chubby little cheeks were evidence of his mother's custard addiction.

He had a shock of dark hair too, which surprised me. I reached out and gently ran my hand across the top of his head, smoothing down his hair – to absolutely no avail. It stuck straight up again, making me laugh.

Laughing felt odd. It sounded odd too as it combined with a stricken sob. I could feel the strength leaving my body as I struggled to keep it together. This just wasn't fair. Nothing was how it was supposed to be.

Hannah grabbed a chair, set it down beside the crib and ordered me to sit down. "Do you want to hold him?" she asked.

I shook my head. "Not yet."

She nodded and I was relieved that she didn't push me. "I'll leave you two alone for a while," she offered. "If you need anything – "

I cut her off with a question that came out sounding more like a rude demand. "You'll tell me when you know how Gabi is?"

"Of course," she said quietly.

It wasn't enough, but it was all she could give me so I let her leave. Once she was gone, I pulled my chair closer to the little plastic box and turned my attention back to my boy. "So," I whispered quietly. "Fancy seeing you here."

***

>The wait for news was excruciating, but it finally came.

A doctor I'd never met before walked into the room, closing the door behind him. Closing the door wasn't a good sign. Closing the door meant he wasn't going to tell me Gabi was awake and waiting to see me.

He introduced himself but I forgot him name in an instant. "Congratulations," he said, peering into the crib. "He's a handsome boy."

"Thank you," I replied listlessly. "How is Gabrielle?"

The doctor clutched his clipboard tight against his chest and hesitated before speaking. That wasn't a good sign either.

"She lost a lot of blood," he explained. "The onset of anaemia and a rapid drop in blood pressure likely induced cardiac arrest."

"But she's fine now, right?"

I no longer cared why it had happened, or even what had happened. I just needed to hear that she was okay.

"She's out of surgery and we've stabilised her," he said mechanically. "She's been moved to ICU."

All of my breath left my body in one loud huff. She was alive. I could deal with everything else because she was still with us. "Thank you," I muttered, dropping my head.

"She's still gravely ill but –"

"But she's still here," I interrupted, letting my emotions get the better of me. "She wouldn't leave us. I knew she wouldn't leave us."

It was a declaration that meant nothing to the doctor. His expression barely wavered. I suspect he'd dealt with this level of heartbreak before, which probably explained his stony expression. "Spend some time getting to know your son," he urged. "Someone will be in to take you up to ICU shortly."

I looked down at my baby. "Thank you."

The doctor left without another word, plunging the room back into total silence.

"I'm sorry she's not here yet," I said to the tiny boy in the plastic box. I put my hand on the top of his head, futilely smoothing down his hair again. "I can't wait for you to meet her…." I cleared my throat as my voice trailed off. "She's been waiting for you for a long time."

That realisation made the days events seem even crueller. I'd spent years drumming it into Charli that the universe doesn't make mistakes – promising her that on any given day, things were exactly how they were supposed to be. I couldn't accept that as true any more. Nothing was how it was supposed to be.

11. HELPLESS

I don't know if Hannah volunteered for the job of escorting me upstairs to ICU or if she drew the short straw. Either way, I was glad she got the job.

She spent the short elevator ride giving me the rundown on what to expect, and urging me not to be alarmed by what I was about to see.

Her pep talk didn't help. Absolutely nothing could prepare me for that room. The first thing that hit me was the noise. The constant beeping of the machines bounced around in my skull as I ventured further into the sterile, unwelcoming room.

Then I saw her.

My beautiful coppery haired Gabs lay motionless on the bed. She barely looked real.

Her porcelain skin was always pale, but the pink flush in her cheeks was gone. Seeing her so lifeless made me wonder if she was really with us at all.

There were leads stuck to her chest, a blood pressure cuff on her arm and probe attached to her finger.

"When will she wake up?" I croaked.

"Any time now," Hannah replied quietly.

"Can I touch her?"

"Of course."

I reached for her hand and gave it a tiny squeeze. I got nothing back, but I was grateful for her warm touch. "We need you, Gabs," I whispered. "Please come back."

"Keep talking to her, Alex," urged Hannah. "She'll wake soon."

I nodded but didn't reply.

"I'm going home now," she added. "Is there anything you need me to do?"

"Yes," I replied. "Can you call Floss? Ask her to call Charli and tell her what's happened. I need her to know."

"Of course."

Politeness and courtesy seem to go out the window in a crisis. So many people had gone up and above for us that day, and I hadn't thanked any of them. Gabi would've been appalled by my bad manners, and truthfully I was too.

I just couldn't do anything about it. I couldn't even think straight. I was consumed by a dreadful combination of helplessness and guilt.

There was nothing I could do to help Gabrielle and I was guilt ridden because I'd left our son in the care of strangers in the nursery. In the four hours since he'd been born, I hadn't even held him – and I hated myself for it.

To make matters worse fatigue was setting in. I slumped forward in my chair, rested my cheek against Gabi's hand, and closed my eyes.

12. DISCONNECTED

"I dreamed about you last night."

I sat bolt upright at the sound of Gabrielle's croaky voice and rushed out her name.

A slow smile crept across her face and she turned her hand palm up, motioning for mine.

I took her hand and brought it to my mouth, kissing her fingers over and over to compensate for the fact that I couldn't find words.

"I dreamt you were in the ocean," she hoarsely mumbled. "Looking for me."

"I've been looking for you for a while, Gabs," I whispered. "I'm glad you're back."

I let go as she slowly pulled away and moved her hand to her stomach. Wonderment turned to confusion and I moved quickly to fill in the blanks. "We have a little boy," I told her.

"He's alright?"

I leaned forward and kissed her upper arm. "He's perfect."

Understandably, she wanted to see him. I turned my head, searching for someone to accommodate her. In my mind it was simple. All they had to do was wheel the baby and his plastic box into the elevator and bring him to his mother.

The nurse who approached us didn't pay much attention to my request. She was more concerned with Gabrielle. "Once you're well enough to leave ICU, you'll join your baby back on the ward," she said, fussing with the bits and pieces that attached Gabi to the machines.

Whether Gabrielle accepted it or not, the massive trauma had slowed her down. There was no angry protest from her. She barely had strength to speak.

Tears rolled from her eyes, saturating her auburn hair. I wanted nothing more than to take her in my arms, but couldn't possibly do it without displacing the equipment she was hooked up to.

"If you need anything, just ask," instructed the nurse.

"I just need my baby," she whispered.

If the nurse heard her, she ignored her. I was grateful when she walked away. The next words out of my mouth probably weren't going to be kind.

I turned my attention back to Gabrielle. "Please don't cry," I begged. "I'll tell you about him."

"You have to," she replied. "I know nothing."

"He's big, Gabs." I smiled at her. "He's going to be a footy player. And he has so much hair," I marvelled. "It sticks straight up on his little head."

Her expression remained blank as she stared up at the ceiling. "You should be with him, Alex."

"They're taking good care of him in the nursery," I assured. "I need to be here with you."

"If I can't be with him, you should be." Her voice was barely stronger than a whisper, but I could still tell she was cross with me. "He needs one of us."

I swept my hand through her hair. It wasn't soft and shiny like it usually was. It was as dull and lank as the rest of her body. "Hurry up and get well and he'll have both of us."

In what looked like a move that took great effort, Gabrielle reached for my hand. I didn't let go until she drifted off to sleep again.

Following Gabi's orders, I ventured downstairs to the nursery while she was sleeping. Pathetically, I didn't even go in. I stood at the big window and watched my little boy from a distance. There were four other babies in the room with him, all settled quietly in their little plastic boxes. I was glad he had company. He'd already spent too much time alone.

"You can go in if you want to." I spun around to see a cheery young nurse smiling at me. "He's nearly due for a feed," she added.

"No, it's fine." I shook my head. "Thank you."

Her frown was slight but noticeable. Clearly she thought I was a jerk too. "If you're nervous about feeding him –"

"I'm not nervous," I cut in. "I'm just exhausted."

She nodded as if she understood, but I knew she didn't. My attitude was unfathomable, even to me. Something deep inside me had snapped under the pressure. I'd gone from feeling hopeful and excited to completely dead inside in the space of a few hours. I didn't connect with him. I felt nothing. And I had no idea what to do about it.

***

After a troubled night's sleep on the chair beside Gabi's bed, I woke with a sore neck and a pounding headache. I slipped out and grabbed a terrible cup of coffee to wake myself up.

Gabrielle was awake when I returned, mercifully looking much more like herself. She was still hooked up to the dreadful monitors but the back of her bed had been raised so she was almost sitting up. The brightest part of her demeanour was her smile.

I leaned across and carefully kissed her, avoiding the wires and lines that were stuck to her chest. "Good morning, beautiful girl," I whispered quietly.

"Hello." Her voice still wasn't right, and nor was her body. She felt very warm to me. I could feel the heat radiating off her.

"How are you feeling?"

"Very sore," she replied, grimacing.

"It'll take time, Gabs," I reasoned.

She might have been sore but she was talkative, which was a good sign. "They let me use a phone. I called my parents."

It was probably a call I should've made myself the day before, but I'd been in no fit state to speak to anyone. Even Charli got the news second hand. I'd noticed three missed calls from her on my phone that morning, and still hadn't called her back.

"The timing was good," she continued. "They're leaving for vacation tonight."

I sat down beside her. "What did you tell them?"

"Not very much." She screwed up her pretty face. "They don't need details. I wouldn't want them to worry. I just told them all is well and baby is here," she explained. "And that he has a lot of hair."

"He does." I smiled. "You'll see him soon."

"The doctor said they'll move me down to the ward tomorrow," she replied. "I cannot wait to meet him, Alex. Have you visited him this morning?"

I wanted to lie and tell her I had, but knew she'd see through me. "Not yet."

"You must," she insisted. "Please Alex. You could take pictures so I can see him."

I truly was useless. I hadn't even thought to take pictures for her. "I'll take pictures, Gabs. I promise."

13. ROCK STAR HAIR

Gabi intermittently slept all morning, but never looked comfortable. I imagine trying to sleep while hooked up to machines would be a hard task for anyone. I just didn't want her to be in any pain and it was hard to watch her knowing she probably was.

By early afternoon, I needed fresh air and a break from the constant beeping machines. I headed downstairs and took an aimless ten minute walk around the car park.

The weather was bitterly cold and the air was crisp and fresh. I needed it. I needed it even more when I noticed Wade Davis's souped up red minivan peel into the car park. It screeched to a halt outside the emergency exit and Wade piled out of the driver's side. I almost smiled when

Jasmine threw open the passenger door and tumbled out.

Wade's hunch had been right. She was squealing like a pig. Even from a distance I could hear every insult she hurled at him.

Wade wasn't ruffled in the slightest. He stood in front of her, taking a backward step with every forward stagger Jasmine took, chanting at her. "No pain, no gain, babes!" He slammed his fist into his hand. "You've got this!"

It was like a poorly scripted infomercial. Not even Jasmine was buying it.

"Get the hell out of my way, you lunatic!" she screamed.

"That's it babes," he foolishly encouraged. "Let it all out."

Jasmine let it all out alright. She came out swinging and clocked him in the side of the head with her giant handbag. It must've been a hard blow because Wade hit the deck.

I probably would've gone to his aid but was beaten to it by a couple of enthusiastic orderlies who came rushing out the door pushing a wheelchair.

That's when I finally gave in and laughed.

Wade was pushed through the emergency room doors in a wheelchair, and his pregnant wife - who was mid labour – walked in behind him.

Despite the ridiculousness, I silently wished them well. Every excited couple that walked through those doors deserved to have things run smoothly.

That was the moment that I realised my boy would soon be rooming with the Davis baby in the nursery. His parents would be proudly gushing over him, while my baby continued the lonely wait for his mother.

***

Considering Jasmine and Wade had been admitted, I was surprised to see Hannah sitting at the nurse's station when I stepped out of the elevator.

"I thought you'd be in the delivery suite with Jasmine," I said, approaching her desk.

Hannah smiled up at me. "She's well taken care of. Someone else has the pleasure of attending that delivery," she replied, sounding totally relieved by the prospect. "Your little man's been waiting for you." She pointed toward the door of the nursery. "You can bathe him if you want to."

I stiffly shook my head. "Gabrielle wants some pictures. I promised her I'd take some for her."

Hannah stood up and walked around the desk. "Okay, you can just sit and hold him for a while," she pressed. "Get to know him a little better."

I deliberated for a quick moment, wondering what she'd think of me if I told her how I really felt. I didn't know her well enough to decide, so I kept quiet.

"Come with me," she urged, grabbing me by the elbow.

Hannah led me through the door and across to the little plastic box closest to the viewing window. My perfect little boy was swaddled firmly in a white blanket, and had a little blue cap on his head.

"Why are you making him wear a hat?" I asked. "He has rock star hair. He should be showing it off."

She gently pulled the hat off his head. "I didn't want him making the bald babies jealous."

I smiled down at my son but made no attempt to touch him.

"Hold him, Alex," she urged. "He needs you."

I lifted my head, forcing myself to look her in the eye. "I'm not much good to him at the moment," I confessed.

"You're here," she stated. "That's all he needs."

"Gabi should be here."

"And she will be – just as soon as she's well enough," she replied. "So in the meantime, it's up to you to hold the fort. You'll just have to enjoy him by yourself for a while."

"I can't bathe him."

"I'll bathe him," she offered. "You can watch."

14. TWO STEPS BACK

I loaded my phone up with a million pictures of my son having his first bath. It wasn't the most relaxing of tasks. The poor little bloke screamed bloody murder the whole time, reminding me of a pissed off little kitten.

His mother had been deathly afraid of the water until I taught her to swim. Judging by the baby's reaction to his first bath, he needed a few swimming lessons in the black river too.

Gabrielle didn't seem to care that there wasn't a decent picture to choose from. "He's so little," she beamed, holding the phone to her face. "And he does have a lot of hair."

The phone was shaking in her hand. I discreetly held her wrist to steady her. "Are you cold, Gabs?"

"No," she insisted, eyes glued to the phone. "I'm fine. When will they take me to see him?"

"Soon, babe," I promised.

"They took more blood from me this morning," she told me. "I'm tired of being poked and prodded. You must tell them I'm fine."

I silently vowed to do no such thing. She was far from fine and her defensive attitude led me to think she knew it too. Calling her out on it would only rile her so I shifted the conversation back to the baby. "He really is cute, Gabs."

She brought the screen closer to her face. "Isn't he?" she gushed. "He doesn't look like a Pierre-Auguste, though."

Thank God.

"No, I don't think he does either."

"He needs a name, Alex."

I totally agreed, but now wasn't the time. Neither of us were in the right frame of mind to be naming a child. It didn't stop Gabi from trying though. She spent the next few minutes brainstorming.

I was actually glad when a doctor walked in and interrupted us. It saved me from having to explain why I thought Lionel was a terrible name for our son.

He introduced himself and asked Gabrielle how she was feeling. She lied and told him she felt great.

He nodded, but obviously wasn't buying it. "Gabrielle, there are some abnormalities in your blood tests," he said seriously. "It indicates an infection."

"I'm perfectly fine," she insisted.

"We're going to administer a course of antibiotics," he continued, ignoring her.

"I'm seeing my baby today," Gabi demanded. "They told me I could see him today."

As far as she was concerned, being ill wasn't a good enough reason to keep her separated from him. My heart broke for her all over again. Try as she might, it was an argument she wasn't going to win.

"We'll concentrate on getting you well again first." The doctor's tone was one of pure pity.

"Then we'll move you downstairs and reunite you with your son."

"Today?" she asked hopefully.

He didn't need to answer. Gabi knew it wasn't going to happen. She burst into tears and I reached for her hand. "Soon, Gabs," I whispered. "You'll be with him soon."

"Not soon." She growled out the words, sounding the strongest she had since the ordeal began. "Today."

It was hard not to feel angry. We were already on the ground, bruised and beaten. I just couldn't understand why the universe kept delivering more kicks.

The doctor left the room and two nurses began fussing with Gabi's IV lines. The tremor in her hands was so bad now that I could barely hold her still.

I felt helpless and scared all over again, and trying to hide it from her wasn't working. "I'm here, Alex," she said quietly.

I brought her shaking hand to my lips. "I'm here too, Gabrielle."

She stopped talking after that. I didn't push her for conversation, and she eventually drifted off to sleep.

***

I couldn't deny that the atmosphere on the maternity ward was much more pleasant than the ICU ward. Every single person I saw looked thrilled to be there. Perhaps it was because they were part of the ninety-nine percent of the population who managed to bring their babies into the world without a hitch. I represented the one percent who resented every single one of them.

"Alex!" called an excited voice from further down the hall.

I didn't have to turn around to know who it was. "Wade," I replied listlessly.

"How's it going, mate?" He slapped me on the back as soon as I was in reach.

I resisted the urge to punch him in the face and forced a polite reply. "Fine."

"Good stuff. Is Gabrielle here too?" I nodded. "Jasmine came in this afternoon. I needed to get out of there for a while. It's getting pretty intense."

I was glad Wade Davis was a self-absorbed fool. He didn't think to ask how Gabrielle was, which saved me from having to explain. "Well, good luck."

"You too," he called as I walked away. "When do you reckon your boy will get here?"

His question was innocent enough, but I was back to fighting the urge to smash him. I turned back to reply. "He's here. He was born yesterday."

"Aww, crap," he huffed. "Jasmine will spew when she finds out you and Gabi beat her to the punch."

"Yeah." I shook my head, trying to shake free of the disgust I was feeling. "We're real winners."

15. LITTLE KITTEN

My little boy was alone in the nursery. All of the other babies were probably hanging out in their mother's rooms. I pulled a chair across to the little plastic box and sat down.

He was wearing the stupid hat again. I gently pulled it off his head and hid it in my pocket. "Sorry about the hat," I said quietly. "Some people have no sense of style."

I lightly rested my hand on his back. Unlike his mum, he felt calm and still. "I think I talked her out of calling you Pierre-Auguste," I said quietly.

I looked up at the clock on the wall. It was nearly six in the evening. My son had been in the world for over thirty hours and hadn't been held by either of his parents. His mother's reasons were valid. Mine weren't and it was getting harder to justify by the minute. I swept my hand through his spiky dark hair. "I'm so sorry, little boy." My voice quaked. "She'll be here soon, I promise."

He stirred and wriggled beneath my hand. I couldn't work out if he was trying to escape the blanket or me. When he started crying, I stupidly panicked and went to find help for my pissed off little kitten.

The first nurse I came across was Hannah. I was always grateful to see her, but especially at that moment.

"Hey, Alex," she greeted.

"Hi." I pointed back at the nursery. "He's crying."

"He's probably getting hungry," she replied. "He eats well, that boy of yours. I'll get you a bottle."

"I can't feed him." I sounded appalled. "Can you do it?"

She frowned. "I could, but you're his dad."

"You're a nurse."

"I am," she agreed. "I help those who are sick or injured or helpless. Which category do you fall under?"

"Helpless." *Hopeless.*

"You've done this before," she reminded. "Why are you so afraid of him?"

There was no point trying to explain something I didn't understand. "Please, Hannah," I begged. "Just feed him for me."

She narrowed her eyes. "If you need help to –"

"I don't need help," I snapped, pointing toward the door. "I need someone to go in there and feed my son."

Hannah Davis was no pushover. She stepped forward, speaking slowly and quietly. "Find a better way of working through this, Alex. This isn't helping."

"Tell me how," I demanded. "If you have the answers, Hannah, I'd love to hear them."

She didn't answer me. Instead, she headed into the nursery to tend to the baby I couldn't deal with.

16. HORROR STORY

I ignored the suggestions of going home in favour of another uncomfortable night in the chair beside Gabi's bed. I managed to grab a shower but feeling refreshed only lasted until I got dressed. I was so bedraggled and worn down that a three-day-old shirt no longer bothered me. The only thing I cared about was being with Gabrielle. Considering they'd been pumping her full of antibiotics for hours, I expected her to be much better by morning.

She wasn't.

If anything, she looked worse. Her skin was pale, she was violently trembling and her hair was damp with sweat.

I reached for her hand, doing my best to appear unaffected by her terrible appearance.

Gabi turned her head in my direction.

"Alright, Gabs?" I asked.

She didn't seem to be looking at me. Her green eyes were drifting without purpose as if she couldn't see a thing. After a long moment of silence, she answered me in French.

"English, Gabrielle," I gently urged. "I don't understand."

She frowned and tried again – in French – and even that didn't sound right.

I straightened up in the chair and called out to a passing nurse. "Something is wrong," I told her. "She's not making any sense."

"We're running more tests," she replied grimly. "We'll know more soon." Her expression led me to think she knew exactly what was going on. She just wasn't prepared to tell me.

"It's not good is it?" I asked, already knowing the answer.

"No," she gently confirmed. "She's very ill."

I looked across at Gabi. Her eyes were still wandering, and so was her mind. I have no idea who she was mumbling to in French, but it wasn't me.

"Oh, Gabs," I whispered in total despair. "What now?"

I didn't recognise a single person in the group who filed into the room a few minutes later, but as usual, they all seemed to know us.

"Mr Blake, I'm doctor Barnard," announced the spokesman.

I didn't reply. I just stared, trying to predict the next words out of his mouth. I knew it wouldn't be good. It was never good.

I was right to be worried. The latest round of tests had confirmed that the infection had spread to Gabrielle's bloodstream. "We're monitoring her very closely," he told me. "Tests on her blood cultures have identified the type of infection we're dealing with, and we're treating her with the correct antibiotics."

The only thing I concluded was that they'd been botching her treatment before now. I was livid. "You mean you've been giving her the wrong ones?"

"It's a delicate balance, Alex," he replied calmly.

I released Gabi's hand and stood up. It was stupid, aggressive and pointless. "Fix her!" I demanded. "She has a brand new baby downstairs who needs her. *I* need her."

Why didn't they know this? Why weren't they doing more?

He ignored my outburst and continued with the horror story. "We're going to place Gabrielle into an induced coma," he explained. "It will give her body a chance to heal."

"No," I snapped, appalled by the idea. "Find another way."

"Gabrielle has sepsis, Alex. She's in the early stages of organ failure. We have no other option at this point."

My heart started beating fast. I'd felt it happen so many times over the past day that I knew exactly what was causing it – pure unadulterated fear.

I had nothing sensible to add to the conversation, so I didn't speak. I just listened as he explained how her already weakened heart was failing again. Her kidneys were packing up too, adding to her massive woes.

I cried when my daughter was born. I cried when my mother died too, but the strangled sob that fell out of my mouth was a sound I'd never made before in my life. I just couldn't deal with anything more. I sat back down and leaned forward, resting my head on Gabi's forearm.

In a move I wasn't expecting, she gripped a fistful of my hair. "*Je suis ici*, Alex."

I don't know how I understood her, but I did. "I'm here too, Gabs," I whispered.

17. BLAKE BABY

Being anywhere near that room while they sedated Gabrielle was never going to happen. Even if I'd wanted to stay, they wouldn't have allowed it. For the second time in three days, I was pushed out the door with a firm hand to the back. I headed downstairs to the maternity ward. I wasn't being a dutiful, caring father. I just had nowhere else to go.

As soon as I stepped out of the elevator, Wade pounced as if he'd been waiting for me. "It's a boy!" he announced gleefully.

"Congratulations," I mumbled, pushing past him.

Wade foolishly stopped me with a hand to my chest. I looked at his hand and then glared at him. It had no effect.

"We called him Lachlan," he boasted. "His name rhymes with the twins'. Clever, eh?"

I was too jumbled to work it out, and didn't care to ask for an explanation. "Genius," I muttered.

He dropped his hand. "Thanks," he crowed. "Sorry to hear about Gabrielle. My gran told me she was in rough shape. Tough break, eh?"

I hadn't laid a punch on someone since I was a sixteen-year-old hothead, but something deep in my soul told me to make an exception. I grabbed a fistful of Wade's shirt and bailed him up against the metal doors of the elevator.

"It's not a tough break," I menaced through gritted teeth. "A tough break is a broken jaw."

I didn't loosen my grip as both of Wade's hands flew up in surrender. He looked terrified but I was beyond caring. I just wanted to hit something, and at that moment, he was it. I might never have released him if Hannah hadn't rushed over and pulled me off him.

"Stop it, Alex!" She dragged me a few steps back by my shirt. "What does this solve?"

"Nothing," I spat. "But it'll make me feel better."

"I'm prepared to forgive you, Alex," announced Wade, shrugging his shirt back into place. "I understand grievery."

"One punch," I growled, taking a quick lurch forward. "Just give me one shot."

"No!" they both yelled in unison.

Hannah ordered Wade to go back to the safety of his family. As soon as he was gone, she spun me around, bunched up my shirt in her hand and pushed me against the wall. I should've known she'd be skilled at pulling people into line. She was the mother of the Lost Boys. "You listen to me," she ordered. "He's an idiot, but he's always been an idiot. Don't take your troubles out on him."

I pulled in a calming breath, giving her enough confidence to release her hold on me. I straightened my shirt as best I could. Nothing was going to make me look neat. I'd been wearing the same shirt for days.

"I'm sorry," I mumbled contritely. "I shouldn't have done that."

"No," she agreed. "Not your brightest moment. How is Gabi this morning?"

I wasn't capable of putting a gentle spin on my reply. "They're putting her into a coma," I said bluntly. "Things are getting worse, not better."

She nodded sadly. "I'm sorry, Alex."

The word 'sorry' had been bounced around too many times in the past couple of days. It was an empty sentiment that meant nothing to me.

"You're a nurse, Hannah," I pointlessly reminded. "You know the score. Don't tell me you're sorry, and don't ask me how she is."

"Okay." She took a step back, completely unruffled by my bad attitude. "I'll ask a different question. How are you?"

"I'm fine," I replied mechanically.

"Good." She pointed to the nursery. "You can go in there and spend some time with your son then."

***

Spending time with the baby was completely different to sitting with Gabrielle. The level of agitation and worry was low, but the feelings of guilt and inadequacy never left me. My son never seemed to notice. He was always placid and calm, except when he was being bathed.

He was awake for a change, wide-eyed and quietly checking out his surroundings through the clear plastic box.

"So, you're alone in here again?" I asked, leaning forward in the chair to peer over the edge of the crib. "I'd be making the most of it if I was you, mate. The Davis kid will be in here soon."

If he was worried by the prospect, it didn't show.

"I wish I had better news for you today," I mumbled. "Your mum isn't doing very well. I don't know what to do."

No one seemed to know what to do. That was the worst part. I certainly wasn't going to get any answers from the baby, but he was a good listener.

"I can't even think straight any more," I confessed. "And today I feel old and tired." I brushed my hand over his dark hair. "That's probably not what you want to hear, huh? If it makes you feel any better, your sister had a rough start too and she turned out okay. I wasn't old and tired then, though. I was just young and stupid."

I'd had no clue what I was doing when Charli was born. I'd bluffed my way through her entire childhood, trying to keep her on track as best I could by grasping anything that would keep me in the little girl loop. I hadn't anticipated ever being ready for another child, mainly because I'd spent years having my arse kicked by the first one.

As frustrating as it was for Gabrielle, the long process of getting pregnant had probably helped ease me back into parenthood. My mind was totally in the game this time around. I was ready and excited – right up until everything went haywire on the day he was born. Now I couldn't even get my act together enough to hold him. It was just too cruel to comprehend.

I sat for a long time, paying attention to every single move he made. Conversation was sparse, but I didn't beat myself up over it. There's a limit to what you can talk about when it's one-sided, and I'd covered a lot of subject matter over the last few days.

My eyes drifted to the card stuck on the end of the crib. Every detail of his short life was written on it. His weight, length, and birthday were correct. His name was only half right. "Blake baby," I said aloud. "That's what they're calling you?"

I tore the card off the crib and headed out to the nurse's station. Hannah didn't notice me swipe a pen off the desk. She was on the phone.

"We need to find you a name, little man," I said, sitting back down beside him. "Blake baby won't do."

I peered down at my son, trying to figure out what to call him. All I knew for certain is that he was no Pierre-Auguste, and Lionel was definitely out of the question. "My little boy in the box," I whispered.

He began to stir and let out a funny little groan. My grand effort to settle him came in the form of a gentle pat on his back. "Okay, okay, I won't call you that any more," I promised. "You could be Jack in the box. What do you reckon?"

As expected, he didn't protest.

I said the name a hundred times in my head, and a couple of times out loud. It wasn't a name Gabi and I had discussed, but I liked it.

I wrote it down on the card. "Just so you know, you're not out of the woods yet. Your mum will probably call you Jacques."

He groaned again, and would probably do so every time his mother put her French spin on his name.

"Jack Blake," I announced, pushing the card back into the slot on the front of the crib. "Perfect, classic and strong."

Hannah poked her head around the doorway. My first instinct was to hide the pen I'd swiped, but she wasn't there to talk stationary.

"I've just had a call from upstairs," she said quietly. "You can go back to ICU if you want to."

I glanced at the clock on the wall. I'd been sitting with Jack for well over an hour. I was almost proud of the accomplishment.

I nodded. "Will you come with me, please?"

"Of course."

"Okay, just give me a minute?"

Hannah smiled briefly. "Take as long as you need."

She closed the door as she left. I hadn't noticed her do that before. Perhaps she thought I didn't need supervision any more.

I half-heartedly fussed with Jack's blankets before gently brushing the back of my hand down his chubby cheek.

"I'll be back soon," I whispered. "Don't go anywhere."

18. CASUAL AND CALM

Hannah dutifully escorted me back to the ICU, just as she'd done the day before. We stepped into the elevator and the doors closed behind us. "She's just going to look like she's sleeping, right?" I asked.

I'd already seen the horrible machines they were monitoring her with. In my mind, there was nothing else they could inflict upon her poor body.

Hannah glanced across at me. "It'll be a little different, Alex," she quietly replied. "You just have to remember that she's not in any pain, okay?"

I managed a stiff nod. I might've even pulled off a calm expression, but I was terrified to the point of nausea.

Moving slower than I'd ever done in my life, I walked from the doorway to Gabi's bed.

It was naïve to think things couldn't get worse. The leads on her chest were still in place, so was the cuff on her arm and the thing on her finger. I could deal with that. What I couldn't deal with was the tube that had been forced down her throat. I asked Hannah what it was. If I'd been thinking clearly, I wouldn't have needed an explanation.

"It's a ventilator," she replied solemnly. "It's helping her breathe."

"Do you think she's going to get better?" I hoarsely whispered.

"She's a fighter, Alex," she replied. "Gabi likes a good fight. Remember when Flynn cut back the bougainvillea on the fence line? I thought she was going to knock him out."

I huffed out a strange noise that could almost have passed as a laugh. "She wanted to," I shakily confirmed. "I held her back with custard."

"You know she'll fight," she encouraged. "You just have to be strong too."

I wondered if I could do it, and quickly realised I couldn't. A scorching wave of heat washed through my whole body. "Hannah," I mumbled. "I think I'm going to be sick."

I got as far as the corridor, put my hands to my knees and doubled over.

Hannah was right behind me. When she thrust a plastic basin under my chin I threw up for the first time in years. I heaved and I sobbed. Then I apologised and heaved some more.

"Vomit doesn't bother me, Alex," she reassured. "I've seen worse."

It bothered me but I didn't have a whole lot of humility left at that point.

After a long few minutes, another nurse appeared. She handed me a warm washcloth. In return, Hannah gave her a bowl of vomit. She slipped away without saying a word. I couldn't even find the strength to thank her.

"You don't have to go back in there if you don't want to," said Hannah.

"I'm fine," I lied. "I'm okay now."

"Is there anything you need me to do?" she asked.

I glanced across at her. "Just look after Jack."

"I like that name." She smiled. "Anything else?"

I shook my head. "No."

She put her hand on my upper arm. "If it gets too much, come back downstairs," she instructed. "I'm rostered on until six if you need me."

***

Heading back into the room was no less traumatic the second time, but at least I managed to do it without throwing up. I sat down next to Gabi's bed and reached for her hand. She didn't feel clammy any more – just warm.

While she was awake I'd tried desperately hard to keep conversation casual and calm. For some reason, I still worked at convincing her that things were okay. "What's going on, Gabs?" I croaked. "You usually shy away from attention. All eyes are on you now, babe."

In a perfect world, she would've woken up and cut me down with one of the French expletives she was so fond of. I even paused to give her time.

That was the moment I noticed that her chest was softly rising and falling in perfect sync with the ventilator.

She was so close to being gone I couldn't stand it. Casual and calm was getting harder to do.

I brought her hand to my mouth. "Please, please don't leave us," I begged. "If I can do better, I will. I'll do anything, Gabi." I laid her hand gently on the bed and rested my forehead against her palm. "Just stay."

I sat with Gabrielle for hours. When I started mentally counting the beeps of the machines, I began to worry that I was losing my mind. Solo conversations tend to make you feel crazy too, and I'd been having a lot of them lately.

"I saw Wade earlier," I told her. "Jasmine had a baby boy. They called him Lachlan." I went on to explain his nonsense rhyming theory, and his ridiculous made up grievery word.

I left out the part about me collaring him at the elevator. It wasn't something I was proud of, and Gabrielle would've been appalled.

I'm not a jealous man, but it was impossible not to feel envious of Jasmine and Wade. Their family was safe and intact. Mine was hurt and hanging by a thread.

Whoever the higher power was who dealt that hand had a lot to answer for.

Charli

19. BABY BROTHER

I'd been secretly planning a trip back to the Cove to meet my baby brother for weeks. All I'd been waiting for was the news that he'd arrived. It was Floss who called me, and the announcement wasn't entirely joyful.

Pressing her for information was useless. She really didn't have any. All she could tell me was that there had been complications.

"The baby is fine," Floss told me. "Gabrielle had some drama, but she's recovering."

I packed my bags while we were talking. Adam booked me a flight online and I was on a plane four hours later.

I'd never been away from Bridget for longer than a night, but the decision to leave her in New York with her dad came easily. The kid wasn't a good traveller. Long haul flights were a nightmare, and trying to cope with four days of jetlag afterwards was worse. I missed them both already but for now, the excitement of meeting my baby brother was winning out over pining.

Being back in Australia was also a treat. The June weather seemed colder than usual after leaving New York in the midst of summer. It was a strange transition, but a lovely reminder that I was back on home soil.

I hadn't managed to get hold of Alex in days, but figured the best place to catch him would be at the hospital. I picked up a cab at the airport and headed straight there.

***

If lugging a heavy bag of luggage through the hospital foyer seemed odd, no one questioned it. I didn't need to ask for directions. I was more than familiar with the maternity ward. I was also familiar with the crotchety nurse that met me as I got out of the elevator.

Nurse Nasty hadn't mellowed in the years since Bridget was born. She hadn't grown an inch either. She was still tiny and mean. "No visitors before one," she barked. "Mothers and babies need their sleep."

I didn't get a chance to plead my case. A nurse swooped in out of nowhere and saved me. "I'll take care of it," she offered. "Leave it with me."

Nurse Nasty nodded stiffly. "See that you do, Micky." She marched off down the corridor in her clunky white orthopaedic shoes.

"Your name is Micky?" I asked, turning to my rescuer.

She grinned. "Short for Michaela."

I smiled back, strangely impressed that I'd met another woman who lived with the pain of being burdened with a boys name – or a mouse's depending on how you looked at it.

"Thanks for saving me," I said appreciatively. "You're really brave."

She was really pretty too. For a quick moment I considered packing her into my suitcase and taking her home to Ryan. No one on earth appreciated gorgeous blondes more than him.

"Her bark is worse than her bite," she assured. "At least that's what they tell me."

"Good to know."

"So who are you here to see?" she asked.

I followed her as she walked toward the nurse's station, dragging my bag behind me. "My brother," I replied. "He's new here."

"Awesome," she beamed. "I don't usually work on the maternity ward. Give me a minute and I'll find out where he is." She sat down at the desk, clicked the mouse and brought to computer screen to life. "What's his mum's name?"

"Gabrielle Décarie."

Micky typed in her name and seemed to spend an eternity reading the screen. When she finally turned her attention back to me her cheerful expression was gone. "She's in ICU."

I forced myself not to panic. I knew there had been complications. Perhaps she'd been sent to ICU to recover. "She's okay though, right?" I asked.

Micky leapt out of her chair. "I'll find someone who can bring you up to speed," she offered. "I've only just come on shift."

She'd dodged my question like a pro, which made me extremely nervous. She then dodged me by taking off down the corridor, but only got as far as the elevator.

Hannah Davis stepped out as the doors opened. I was relieved to see her. The maternity ward was her stomping ground. If anyone would know what was going on, it was her.

Micky obviously thought so too. Even from a distance, the conversation looked tense, and when she pointed back at me, I was sure I wasn't going to enjoy being brought up to speed.

I used the minute alone to try calling Alex. It went straight to voicemail, just as it had every time I'd tried calling him in the past few days.

I ended the call as Hannah approached and tried my best to greet her with a smile. I hadn't seen her in six months so it seemed like the polite thing to do. "How are you, Hannah?" I asked.

She nodded, and quickly moved on from the pointless pleasantries. "Have you spoken to your dad today?" she asked.

"No." I pointed to my luggage. "I just got off a sixteen hour flight."

She nodded again, frowning this time. "Do you want to take a seat?" She pointed to a small lounge area to my left. "We'll have a chat."

I followed Hannah's lead and sat down on the small sofa, and she wasted no time in getting down to business. The no-nonsense way she explained Gabrielle's condition left no room for misinterpretation. The Parisienne was in dire straits. "The next twenty-four hours are crucial," she said gently. "We'll know more tomorrow."

I read between the lines whether I was supposed to or not. "She could die?"

"She's a fighter, Charli," she replied ambiguously. "You know that."

I wondered how much fight it took to stay alive when your body was hell bent on shutting down. It was impossible to get my head around.

Gabrielle was young and fit. She was also a Décarie. That alone meant that she would've played by every pregnancy rule in the book to ensure her baby got here safely.

She'd been a tyrant while I was pregnant. Alex had saved me from her wrath more than once after being sprung eating cereal for dinner. Alex's approach had been much more laid back. His whole approach to life was laid back. It made me wonder how he was dealing with this nightmare. "How's my dad?" I asked.

"He's not coping very well," replied Hannah. "With Gabi or the baby."

I expected to hear that he was overtired and distraught. I wasn't expecting to hear that he'd barely had anything to do with the baby. When Bridget was born he'd been attentive and loving and desperate to see her. "He's never held him?" I asked, almost certain I'd misheard her.

"I've tried to push the issue a few times, but he just gets irate," she explained.

My thoughts turned to the tiny little boy whose entrance into the world had been so rough and traumatic. He deserved so much more than he'd had so far.

I stood up. "Where's my brother?"

Hannah pointed toward the nursery.

"I need to be with him," I replied, already heading for the door.

"You're not supposed to be in there, Charli," said Hannah quietly. "Only parents are – "

I rudely cut her off as I turned back. "Where are his parents, Hannah?" I asked, throwing my arms wide. "The way I see it, I'm all he's got right now."

She pointed at the door again. "Go," she permitted. "You're fine."

I wasn't fine. I was as scared as I'd ever been, but I didn't want the baby to pick up on my angst. I somehow slowed my roll and calmed myself down before going in.

I'd often wondered what he'd look like. I'd also wondered whether he'd be feisty like Gabrielle or calm like Alex. I quickly decided that the little bundle who was fast asleep in the plastic crib was a hundred percent his father's son. He didn't wake when I scooped him up. He didn't even stir when I brushed my hand over his head, admiring his lovely spiky dark hair. The kid couldn't have cared less that his only sister had just travelled ten thousand miles to meet him.

"Hey." I tickled his cheek. "I've come to visit you. Wake up."

It was the brightest of moments on an otherwise dark day. I felt a hundred emotions surge through me as I cradled the newest addition to my family, and for a quick minute not one of them was sad.

"What's your name?" I asked quietly. Hoping for a clue, I looked at the card on the crib. In messy scrawl that I instantly recognised as my father's was the answer. I uncurled his little fingers and held his hand. "Hello, Jack," I whispered. "I'm Charli, your sister."

I sat down on the nearest chair and loosened his blanket. Holding him was the biggest support I could offer, and I was prepared to do it indefinitely. Cradling him close to my chest, I promised him a hundred times that everything was going to be fine. Then I prayed to God that I wasn't lying.

20. FAITH

From what Hannah had told me, Alex rarely spent time with the baby voluntarily. When he appeared at the doorway of the nursery less than half an hour after I arrived, I knew she must've sent for him.

He looked awful – so bad that I burst into tears at the sight of him. His usually bright brown eyes were bloodshot and his face looked drawn and tired. He was a mess, inside and out.

"Don't cry, Charli," he mumbled. "Please."

I lowered the baby into his crib and grabbed a handful of tissues from a nearby change table. "I can't help it," I replied, keeping my back turned. "I've just met my little brother. It's overwhelming."

Jack wasn't the reason for my tears, and Alex knew it. "That's one way of describing the events of the past few days," he muttered.

Confident that I'd pulled myself together, I turned back to face him.

Alex's face was completely expressionless, and he hadn't ventured any further than the doorway. "Why are you here?" he asked. "How did you know to come here?"

"I'd always planned to visit once Jack was born," I replied. "I caught the first flight out after Floss called me."

He nodded, but gave me nothing else.

"How is Gabrielle?" I repeated.

Alex brought his hand to his face, drawing invisible circles around his mouth with his finger. "She has a tube down her throat," he replied on the brink of tears. "I can't bear seeing her like that."

Every single reply I built in my head was trite and cliché, and he didn't need to hear any of them. I swung the conversation in a different direction instead. "You look like a derro, Alex." I pointed at his dishevelled shirt. "Gabs would flip out if she saw the state of you."

Alex looked down at his shirt and huffed out one hard laugh. "I don't care. I can't hold it together any more, Charli."

He then broke down and cried.

My father had seen me hysterical a million times, but I'd never even seen him shed a tear before that moment. I put no thought into my next move. I rushed over to him and threw my arms around him. "You don't have to," I promised. "I'll hold you together."

***

Being there was really the only contribution I could make, and I quickly worked out that the biggest relief for Alex was that Jack now had company.

I paid careful attention to how he interacted with him. He was jittery and had trouble staying still, which meant Jack lost out in favour of pacing aimlessly around the room. Trying to calm him was pointless, but I tried. "Everything will work out, Alex. Just have faith."

"Faith in what, Charli?" He spun back to face me. "Throwing it out to the universe isn't working for me this time. Nothing is working."

"She's strong," I mumbled. "Be hopeful."

Alex was right upon me now, towering over me as if he was fighting the urge to knock me off my chair. "How can I be hopeful? They cut her baby out of her belly. They've driven needles up her arms. They've pumped her full of drugs. They shoved a tube down her throat, Charli." He was so worked up that he had to pause for breath. "She looks awful and pale and when I hold her hand I can't feel her touch me back. So don't tell me to be hopeful. I don't want to hear that from you."

As hard as it was, I forced myself to look up at him. "What do you want to hear from me?" I asked calmly. "What can I say?"

Alex walked over to the nearest chair and slumped down, resting his elbows on his knees and burying his face in his hands. "Nothing. I'm sorry," he muttered. "I didn't mean to snap at you."

After a long moment, he lifted his head but didn't get a chance to speak again. Jasmine and Wade walked into the nursery, wheeling the newest addition to their family in ahead of them.

Both stopped dead in their tracks. Jasmine looked shocked to see me but for some reason, Wade looked terrified – so terrified that he mumbled something to Jasmine and disappeared out of the room without so much as a hello.

Alex stood. "I'm going back upstairs."

My father's tolerance for the Beautifuls was low at the best of times, but he was usually much more polite about it. I felt the need to apologise to Jasmine once he'd gone.

"It's okay," she replied. "I feel bad for him."

Word travels fast. I wasn't surprised that she already knew what was going on, but the last thing I wanted to do was discuss it with her. I turned my attention to her new baby instead. The Davis baby was much smaller than Jack, and completely bald – but undeniably cute. "He's lovely," I complimented, peering into his crib.

"Yes," she agreed simply. "I brought him in here so I could get some sleep."

I nodded and looked across at my brother. "Jack will be glad to have company."

"It's good that you're here, Charli," said Jasmine. "You're probably needed."

She didn't elaborate, for which I was grateful. On the off chance that she started asking questions, I made up an excuse to leave the room. "It's been a long day for me. I might try and hunt down a cup of coffee."

I'd almost made it to the door when Jasmine called me back. "I didn't bring him in here because I need sleep." She motioned to her son with a small nod. "I'm getting my hair done so we can take some nice photos." Nothing about the confession shocked me, but her meek demeanour was confusing. "You must think I'm really lame."

I shrugged but didn't reply. Lame was one of the nicer words I'd used when summing up Jasmine and her skewed outlook on life.

"I'm really sorry for what your family's going through right now," she quietly added. "I can't imagine how horrible it must be. Can you let Alex know that Wade isn't upset with him?"

I frowned, confused. "Why would he be?"

"Alex nearly thumped him this morning," she casually explained. "Hannah had to break it up."

No wonder Wade had looked so terrified. I'd seen Alex's frustration firsthand that day. Hannah Davis had probably saved his life.

"Alex isn't himself," I defended. "He's under a lot of pressure."

Jasmine nodded.

I was content to leave it at that. I checked on Jack one last time before making my way back to the door.

"Why did this happen, Charli?" Jasmine asked. "Gabrielle didn't do anything wrong."

For once, she wasn't fishing for information. Her concern was genuine.

Perhaps that's why I took the time to answer her. "She has an infection," I explained. "No one knew until it was too late."

"I've had three babies," she said, gazing down at her boy. "Nothing ever went wrong."

I'd never known Jasmine to have an empathetic bone in her body, which highlighted just how unfathomable the situation was. Two women had travelled exactly the same road within hours of each other. Both delivered baby boys. One was now preparing to get her hair done while the other fought for her life. Trying to make sense of it was pointless so I didn't even try. "Luck of the draw, I guess."

I'd spent many years trying not to show weakness where Jasmine was concerned. Breaking down in front of her wasn't an option. I didn't have it in me. I walked out the door without another word, managing to hold it together until I got all the way outside. Then I cried, and I couldn't have cared less who saw me.

21. POEMS

I'd never been in a position of having to take charge where Alex was concerned. I had no idea how to handle him.

First and foremost he needed food and sleep. When he reappeared back in the nursery I demanded that we go home for the night and come back in the morning. He was so shattered that he didn't even protest, even when I commandeered his car keys and told him I was driving.

I wasn't tired at all. Long haul flights usually kick my arse but Adam had booked my flight. Not even I could deny that travelling first class has its merits. I'd slept most of the way and had arrived feeling rested.

It was a quiet journey home to the Cove. The winter weather was calm and clear, unlike my thoughts.

Alex's mind was busy too. At first he only spoke when I asked him a question. By the time we arrived home, he'd stopped replying at all.

***

It didn't take me long to realise that bringing Alex back to the house might not have been the best move. It was a giant reminder of how things were supposed to be.

I tried my best to ignore the bassinette set up in the lounge room, which was difficult. What I really wanted to do was tell him how perfect it looked. It was fussy and frilly and totally impractical. It had Gabrielle's French princess chic stamp all over it.

Alex walked straight through to the kitchen and headed to the fridge.

While his back was turned, I scooped pile of perfectly folded little clothes off the table and carried them down to the baby's room.

I'd been happy to surrender my childhood room to my brother. It was the best room in the house. Even on cold days, the west facing window always caught the warmth of the setting sun. It was also the easiest to sneak out of. If raised the right way, the sash window opened silently. I figured Jack would probably appreciate that detail in fifteen years or so.

For now, he had plenty of other details to concentrate on, namely the magnificent mural on the wall. Every detail was perfect, but Gabi had clearly taken a bit of creative license when it came to depicting the animals.

The multicoloured birds and mauve turtle confused me so much that I moved closer to the wall in a bid to understand it better.

"They're crows," said Alex making me jump.

I dropped the stack of clothes into the cot and turned to face him.

"Really?"

"Yeah. Gabi thought they'd be less creepy if they were different colours."

I couldn't help smiling. "And are they?" I asked curiously.

He leaned against the doorway and folded his arms. "They're still crows."

I turned my attention to the wall. "And what about the purple turtle? I didn't realise you were afraid of turtles too."

"I'm not," he replied dully. "Gabi is."

I didn't bother asking why. The Parisienne's logic was even more skewed than mine at times. "Well, I think it's fabulous," I complimented. "Jack will love it."

It should've been a light-hearted, funny conversation, but Alex shifted it in an instant. "She painted eight of them," he told me. "What does the eighth crow in the poem mean?"

I glanced back at him, frowning. "Why?"

"Because I'm looking for magic, Charlotte," he replied insincerely. "Give me something to work with."

I'd spent a great deal of my childhood taunting him with the silly crow nursery rhyme.

It was sinister and dark and had nothing to do with magic.

"One for sorrow, two for mirth," he prompted, intent on torturing himself. "Tell me the rest."

He wasn't going to let it go so I did as he asked, keeping my voice even as I prepared for the fallout. "Three for a wedding, four for a birth."

"Go on," he ordered, annoyed by my pause.

"Five for silver, six for gold. Seven for a secret, not to be told. Eight for heaven – "

"Eight for heaven," he repeated, cutting me off.

"It's just a silly rhyme, Alex," I mumbled. "It doesn't mean anything."

He wouldn't have looked any more pained if I'd struck him. "You're absolutely right." He choked out the words. "None of it means anything and I'm sorry I spent so many years telling you otherwise."

Before I had a chance to reply, Alex walked out of the door. I heard the back door slam a few seconds later and the familiar sound of splitting wood a minute after that.

22. CRISIS

In times of crisis, people look for meaning. Alex's biggest problem was that he couldn't find one. His whole faith had taken a pounding because the theory that bad things don't happen to good people no longer rung true.

I stood on the edge of the veranda and watched as he took his frustration out on the woodheap. I knew it wasn't a pace he could maintain for long. He was exhausted before he even began.

As soon as he paused, I called out to him. "There's still joy to be found, Alex. Gabi would want you to spend time with Jack," I said strongly. "It's not right that he spends so much time alone."

Alex glanced across at me before raising the axe over his head and belting it down full force, obliterating the wood in front of him. "Don't tell me what Gabi would want."

"I'm not," I insisted. "I'm telling you what Jack wants."

"Don't tell me that either," he snapped.

The horrible situation he was facing had nothing to do with the baby. Pointing it out was harsh but necessary. "Stop punishing him," I demanded. "It's not his fault. He deserves more from you."

In what seemed like slow motion, Alex dropped the axe as if he no longer possessed the strength to hold it. There aren't words to describe how it felt to see my father brought to his knees by nothing more than the cold, hard truth.

"You have to talk to me, Alex," I coaxed desperately. "I can't help you if you don't talk to me."

He didn't move. I got the impression it was a position he could've maintained indefinitely, but at least he found words. "You'll hate me, Charli," he warned.

"I could never hate you."

Alex finally lifted his head and looked across at me. "I wouldn't choose him." The words came out in a strangled sob. "If I could wind the clock back so he never happened, I would. Now tell me you don't hate me."

I'd promised to be the one to hold him together but I was beginning to realise just how ambitious that pledge was. He was unravelling before my very eyes, and I had no idea how to stop it.

"I don't hate you, but you've got to understand something," I said strongly. "Gabi would choose Jack. She'd endure all this and ten times more if it meant getting her baby here safely."

Alex slowly levered himself to his feet as if he was damaged. It proved just how exhausted he was, and how heavy his heart must've been. "She can't endure much more, Charli. That's the problem."

However unfair it might've been, I could feel myself getting frustrated with him. It was so unlike Alex to take on such a defeatist attitude. "What do you hear when the doctors talk to you?" I asked exasperatedly. "Once the antibiotics take effect, Gabrielle's condition will improve." My mouth had got the better of me again. It was a naïve and callous summation that came out sounding heartless and cruel.

Alex threw his head back and groaned in disgust. "What do you imagine when you think of her laying there in a coma, Charli?" he asked angrily. "That she's sleeping peacefully while the Disney bluebirds fly around and draw back her bedcovers?"

"No," I mumbled.

"My heart pounds every time I walk through that door because she always looks worse than the last time." He thumped his hand against his chest. "So forgive me if hope is slipping."

"I'm sorry," I replied remorsefully.

"Don't be sorry," he muttered. "Just think before you speak. And if you can't do that, just be quiet."

23. SAFE PLACES

I wanted to run. If I'd gone with my usual MO and hired a car at the airport, I probably would've done it. Then I would've turned around and come straight back again because Alex needed me. It just didn't feel like it.

Looking after his emotional wellbeing was impossible, and trying seemed to damage to both of us. I decided to work on his physical wellbeing instead.

Thanks to Floss Davis, the fridge was full of food. There were enough dodgy vegan dishes to feed the whole Cove, and not one of them looked appealing.

I finally settled on something I guessed was vegetable soup.

While Alex was in the shower, I heated it up and set the table. For the tiniest moment, it was just like old times – right up until he reappeared in the kitchen and told me he wasn't hungry.

"I'm not leaving until you eat something," I grumbled.

Alex pulled out a chair and sat down. "Where are you going?"

Ignoring the fact that it looked like muddy dishwater, I set a bowl of soup down in front of him and ordered him to eat. "I thought I'd stay at the cottage. You don't have a spare bed here anyway."

That wasn't my main reason for wanting to escape, but he didn't need to know differently.

Alex nodded. "This hasn't exactly been a good homecoming for you, has it?"

"I'm always happy to spend time with you."

"I miss you every day," he said, absently dragging his spoon through his cloudy soup. "All of you."

I pulled out a chair and sat down. "Even Adam?"

He glanced up and flashed a tiny but genuine smile. "A little," he confessed. "But there's no point telling him. I'll deny it."

I laughed, and after a day of immense sadness, it felt good to take a step back for a minute. I could only assume that Alex felt the same way. We sat at the table long after the soup had gone cold, talking about everything except Gabrielle and Jack.

I told him about Bridget's fascination with Central Park, my great new position at the gallery, and Adam's job at his father's firm. "I don't think he really likes it," I explained, "But he's sticking it out."

"He doesn't belong in New York any more, Charli," replied Alex.

I shrugged. "Time will tell, I guess."

"Are you still coming home for Christmas?"

I smiled across at him. "I hope so. I think it'd be great for Bridget and Jack to spend time together."

"Gabi would like that too." His voice trailed off at the mention of her name and in the blink of an eye we were back to square one.

I stood up and carried our bowls to the sink, purely to avoid the woeful expression on his face. It should've been the moment that I came up with something supportive to say, but I'd been shot down too many times for trying.

"Can you drive me to the cottage, please?" I asked quietly.

"Just take my car," he offered. "You can bring it back in the morning."

"Okay."

He lifted his head to look at me. "Do you think things will be better tomorrow, Charli?"

I wasn't prepared to promise anything that could backfire on me later. I was married to the king of tactful ambiguity so I'd learned a thing or two when it came to dodging difficult questions. "If you get some sleep tonight, I guarantee the story of the day will be brighter," I replied.

Alex pushed his chair back and stood up. I didn't move. I was too busy steeling myself for another snarky reprimand.

Thankfully, it didn't come. He walked over and wrapped his arms around me instead. "I'm glad you're here," he murmured, kissing the top of my head.

Nothing compared to a hug from Alex. It was strong and warm and honest. After all these years, it was still the safest place on earth – and I wanted nothing more than for Jack to find his way there too.

24. TAKE YOUR WIFE TO WORK DAY

I didn't feel tired until I got to the cottage. Once I walked through the door and kicked off my shoes, the familiar feeling of being home hit me like a tonne of bricks.

Not one thing looked out of place. It looked exactly as it had when we lived there, only tidier thanks to the absence of toys and the little girl who loved to strew them all over the lounge room.

I didn't spend too much time looking around. It made me think of my little family that were impossibly far away from me.

I found some linen in the cupboard, made up the bed, and spent the next few minutes trying to work out how to make a video call on my phone.

I'd promised Bridget I'd figure it out and call her every morning.

After a lot of messing around, a weird chiming noise rang out. A few seconds later, Adam's handsome face appeared on the screen and I instantly knew I'd called too late to catch Bridget. He was sitting at his desk in his office, and it wasn't even 9AM.

"Hi," he beamed. "You worked it out."

"Was there ever any doubt?"

He pinched his thumb and forefinger together. "Little bit," he replied making me smile.

"Why are you at work so early?"

Adam propped his phone up on something on his desk and began shuffling papers around. "I had a bit of work to catch up on because I wasn't here yesterday," he explained.

"Where were you yesterday?"

He stopped shuffling papers and leaned closer to the screen to whisper to me. "Bridge and I dropped you off at the airport and then hit the town." He wiggled his eyebrows up and down making me laugh. "We did the whole shebang –

the park, the toy stores and lunch. She has four new girls and a new appreciation for chicken nuggets."

My heart suddenly ached, acutely aware that parts of it were missing. "I miss you both."

"We miss you too, Coccinelle," he replied. "How are things in the pretty part of the world?"

I wasn't quite sure how to explain, or even if I wanted to. Adam was oblivious to the events of the past few days. I'd given him nothing more than a quick text message from the airport letting him know I'd arrived.

I eased into it by starting with the good part. Talking about Jack wasn't difficult. "He's big for a newborn," I told him. "Much bigger than Bridget was."

His smile brightened to Décarie level. "She was tiny," he agreed.

"I love your face, Adam," I said irrelevantly.

He leaned back in his chair and straightened his tie. "How about my tie, Charlotte? Do you love my tie?"

The green and blue striped tie had been a gift from the queen. It was hideous. "No," I replied. "But you hate that tie too."

"I do," he confirmed. "But my daughter picked it out for me this morning. She also made my lunch."

"She did?"

He grinned again. "Yeah. Her mama told her to look after me."

"What did she make you?"

"I'll show you." He leaned to the side and pulled open a drawer before dumping a pink Barbie lunchbox on the desk and flipping open the lid. "Peanut butter and mayonnaise sandwiches," he proudly announced.

"Really?"

"Yeah, and an egg." He wasn't even lying. He waved it at the screen to prove it.

I giggled so hard that my stomach hurt, and for a moment, the good pain eased the bad. "How are you supposed to eat an egg?"

"I'm not entirely sure, but she thought to pack a fork," he replied, holding it up to show me. "She's very thoughtful, that daughter of yours."

The silly long-distance conversation took me all the way home, if only momentarily. The instant I broached the subject of Gabrielle, life got serious again.

Adam didn't say a word as I explained the situation. "Things will be better tomorrow," I predicted. Playing it down didn't seem fair but neither did causing unnecessary worry. "Once the antibiotics take effect, I'm sure she'll improve."

Adam frowned. "Gabrielle spoke to Aunt Monique after the baby was born," he told me. "That's how the family found out he was here."

"No one knew she was sick until the next day," I explained. "Things went downhill quickly."

"Did Alex think to call her?" His frown morphed into a concerned stare. "Charlotte, I don't think her parents know any of this."

I sat bolt upright in bed, horrified by the realisation that he was probably right. Alex was in no fit state to deal with anyone. Calling Gabrielle's parents probably didn't even enter his mind. "Adam, you need to call them," I instructed. "Today, okay?"

"I will," he assured. "I'll do it now."

"Will you call me back?" I wasn't ready to let him go, and sounded desperate because of it.

He smiled again as if he knew I needed to see it. "Don't hang up." He picked up the phone on his desk and began dialling. "It'll only take a minute."

Even the longest conversation only takes a minute in French. I had no chance of understanding what he was saying, but he was right when he said it'd be quick. The call only lasted a few seconds. "It went to voicemail," he told me. "I left a message asking her to call me back."

I laid my head back on the pillow. "Okay," I replied dully.

I refused to allow myself to think worst-case scenario. I had to believe that tomorrow Gabi would be better and there would be no need to tell her parents anything.

"Are you tired, Coccinelle?" he asked. "It must be late there."

"Nearly eleven, I think," I replied. "I'm not sure if I can sleep without you, Adam. It's been a long time."

Adam picked up the phone and held it closer to his face. "I'll spend the night with you, Charlotte." The low tone he used was most unfair. "Just go to sleep. I'll keep working and you go to sleep."

"Really?"

"Yeah," he drawled, stretching out the word. "We'll call it Bring Your Wife To Work Day."

"What if I snore?" I joked.

He looked to the screen and smiled. "I'll mute you."

I turned on my side, pulling the blankets up to my chin. Adam set the phone back on the desk and began sifting through papers again.

"You have an answer for everything, Boy wonder."

"Not everything." He was only half paying attention to me as he wrote something down. "Yesterday Bridget asked me why squirrels are so mean. I had no answer for her."

He still would've tried, because that's what we do. We were the parents of the most inquisitive, astute and determined little person on the planet. In order to keep her that way, we had to endure mayonnaise sandwiches and questions about mean squirrels.

It already felt like months had passed since I'd held her in my arms. I took heart in the fact that I had Jack as a proxy cuddler. I also took heart in the fact that I was a stand-in cuddler for him. There was no substitute for being in Adam's arms though, and after just one day, I was already feeling the loss.

I brought my phone closer to my face, studying the handsome man on the screen. "I love you, Adam," I declared. "And your ugly tie."

His dark chuckle was quiet and low. "You're beautiful," he told me. "Now go to sleep or I'll mute you."

I was too tired and heavyhearted to argue. I propped the phone up on the edge of the pillow next to me and watched Adam going about his working day until sleep took me away.

25. TOKEN LOST BOY

Winter in Pipers Cove always seemed to have a tinge of anger to it. The weather was never merely rough. It was punishing.

The thick grey skies weren't always a dependable sign of rain. They were constantly gloomy. Perhaps that's why the Lost Boys were so caught off guard by the early morning downpour.

I was standing on the veranda checking out the surf when the heavy rain flushed the three little boys out of their hiding spots in my garden.

"G'day, Charli," crowed Tyler, shaking his blonde mop of hair like a wet dog.

His swagger made me laugh. All three of Hannah's sons were blessed with great confidence, and it never went to waste. In a move reminiscent of a football tackle, Mason and Sean stormed the porch and threw their arms around me. "We knew you'd come back," beamed Sean.

Tyler played it a little cooler than his brothers. He chose to hang back on the lawn and get pelted by the rain. "When did you get here?" he asked.

"Yesterday," I replied, prising Mason off my leg. "I came to meet my baby brother."

"By yourself?"

I rolled my eyes at the predictable question. "Yes. Adam and Bridget stayed behind in New York."

His cheeky grin transcended the rain. "You should leave them there and stay here for good."

I ignored him for obvious reasons.

"So what have you been up to since I left?" I asked, aiming the question at all three of them.

"We've got a slingshot," announced Shawn, reaching into his back pocket.

"Leave it, Sean," muttered Tyler. "Don't show her."

I smirked across at the oldest boy. "Why can't I see it?"

Tyler finally escaped the rain and stepped up onto the porch, but only to snatch the slingshot from his brother. "It's not very good," he muttered. "Alex told us to shorten the strap, but it still sucks."

I held out my hand. "Let me see."

After a long moment of deliberation, Tyler finally handed it over. "Don't use it," he warned. "You'll get hurt."

I cocked an eyebrow. "I've used one before."

My slingshot phase at ten-years-old was short but memorable. After weeks of begging Alex to make me one, he finally gave in. Things went well for an hour or two until I smashed out my bedroom window – from the inside. My father promptly confiscated it and I hadn't seen it since.

"It's dangerous," claimed Mason. "It hits your face."

The visual demonstration he gave was epic. Mason smacked himself in the eye, groaned exaggeratedly and dropped to the floor.

I turned my attention back to Tyler. "Give me a gumnut," I demanded.

He showed no sign of giving in but Sean caved instantly. He stepped forward and handed me a gumnut from his pocket.

"Don't do it, Charli," warned Mason, still flat out on the deck. "It'll hurt you."

I loaded the nut, lined up my shot and let fly. In a move I couldn't have repeated if I tried, it crossed the yard and pinged against the metal letterbox.

Mason jumped to his feet. "Whoa! Good shot, Charli."

Tyler frowned at me. "Go again," he ordered.

I wasn't keen to give it another shot, mainly because the first one had been a total fluke. I just didn't want the Lost Boys to know.

I called his bluff and handed it back to him. "You do it."

Sean handed Tyler a nut and there was no going back. He moved to the edge of the porch and lined up his shot. The second he drew back the strap, I yelled at him to stop. "Jesus, Tyler!" I snatched it from him. "No wonder it hits you in the face."

His technique was terrible, and downright dangerous. I stood behind him, gave him back the slingshot and talked him through firing it. "Pull it back against the side of your cheek, use the fork in the sling to align your sight."

Surprisingly he did as he was told.

"Now when you release, follow through with your wrist. That way, you won't get hit in the face."

I dropped my hold on him and took a step back. Tyler glanced back at me, looking a little nervous.

"You can do it, Ty," I encouraged.

Whether he believed me or not, he fired. He didn't hit anything, but he didn't hit himself either.

"That was awesome!" The only thing louder than his gleeful yell was the screams of approval from his brothers. "Where did you learn to do that?"

"My dad taught me."

"Your dad is awesome," crowed Sean.

"He is," I agreed.

The Lost Boys fascination with shooting projectiles was carried out completely on the sly. Hannah and Flynn probably would've been appalled to know they'd made a slingshot. I wasn't sure that I'd done the most responsible thing by encouraging them.

Not only was I a bad influence, I was also a coward. When I caught sight of Flynn wandering across the yard, I snatched the slingshot from Tyler and hid it behind my back.

I was now a token Lost Boy.

The rain had stopped so Flynn wasn't in a hurry. It seemed to take forever for him to reach us. By the time he stepped up onto the porch, my guilty heart was smashing against my ribcage.

"Hi, Charli," he greeted.

"Hey."

"Hannah mentioned you were back," he said. "How long are you in town for?"

"Not long," I replied, tightening my grip on the contraband weapon. "Just until Gabi is back on her feet."

He nodded and followed up with a sympathetic smile. "Yeah, I was sorry to hear she's not well."

"She'll be fine," I insisted.

Awkward conversations between Flynn and I were nothing new. I'd always had trouble dealing with him. Clearly not much had changed.

"Well, I just came over to get the boys." He glanced across at them. "Your mum wants you out of the rain, fellas."

Sean and Mason said a quick goodbye and scuttled home. Tyler – true to form – played it much cooler. "I'll see you later, Charli," he said, slowly ambling across the lawn.

"Yeah, okay." I looked across at Flynn. "I've got to go too. I've got to pick Alex up. We're off to see Gabi and the baby."

"Of course," Flynn replied. "Give them my best."

"I will."

If I'd turned around, the jig would've been up so like a total dick, I backed toward the door.

Flynn put me out of my misery early. "Do you want me to take the slingshot with me or do you want Tyler to come back for it?" he asked.

The frigid morning air wasn't enough to dull the heat in my cheeks as I handed it over. "What's the charge?" I asked dully.

Flynn laughed. "Contributing to the delinquency of minors, probably," he teased.

"From what I can work out, they've had it for a while," I told him. "You might want to teach them how to use it safely."

I was in no position to be offering parenting advice, but Flynn didn't seem too outraged. "Hannah would go nuts if she knew. I was happy to let them have their fun in secret."

I shrugged. "It's a dangerous secret."

He half waved the slingshot at me. "I'll keep a better eye on them," he promised. "This parenting gig is tough."

I couldn't help laughing at the pained look on his face.

Adam and I had ended up on the parenthood road by accident. Others spend years preparing for it like Gabi and Alex, and some get the whole kit and caboodle at once like Flynn.

It occurred to me that no one ever perfected the craft. There were just too many variables, and the past few days were case in point.

"Don't give up, Flynn," I encouraged. "One day we might all get the hang of it."

26. OH, MICKY

A good night's sleep had done Alex the world of good. His mood was infinitely brighter when I arrived at the house to pick him up. He was also less jittery and more relaxed – so relaxed that he took the time to walk around his car and survey for damage.

"I didn't hit anything," I said dryly.

He leaned down and brushed his hand against the front bumper. "Are you sure?" he teased.

"Positive." I dangled his bunch of keys at him. "It handles like a tank, though. The Ute was a much prettier drive."

He snatched the keys from me. "There was nothing pretty about my Ute. It was manly and loud."

It must've nearly killed him to give up his beloved Ute in favour of a more family friendly car. It didn't stop me teasing him though. "Unlike this girly thing," I mocked. "Before you know it, you'll be trading it in for a minivan."

He threw open the driver's door. "Get in the girly car, Charlotte," he ordered. "And put your seatbelt on."

We were well out of town before I braved the subject of Gabrielle and Jack. Unlike the day before, Alex wasn't snappy at the mention of their names. If anything, he was optimistic. "Hopefully, she'll be much better today," he told me. I glanced across at him and smiled. "Today will definitely be better."

As far as I was concerned, it already was.

***

There was a lot going on when we stepped out of the elevator on the maternity floor. Yesterday it was quiet and orderly like a hospital should be. Today it resembled a busy hotel lobby. A big pile of luggage was stacked up near the desk at the nurse's station and Wade Davis stood at the counter. I was hopeful that meant that Jasmine and her new baby were checking out.

I muttered to Alex from the corner of my mouth as we walked toward the nursery. "Be nice."

Wade's whole beefy body went rigid at the sight of him. "Alex," he muttered, greeting him with a stiff nod.

Alex surprised both of us by replying. "How are you Wade?"

I couldn't blame him for the look of terror on his face. From what little I knew, my father had threatened to knock him out the day before.

"I'm okay," he replied. "We're going home today."

"Nice." Alex almost managed to sound sincere. "Good luck with everything."

Wade's mouth fell open as if he was going to return the sentiment, but thought better of it. Alex wouldn't have heard him if he had. He'd already disappeared into the nursery.

"I'm very sorry about yesterday. Alex is too," I embellished.

"No worries, Charli," he replied, relaxing in an instant. "I understand."

I wasn't sure that he did, but I smiled and thanked him anyway. I then excused myself and followed Alex into the nursery before he had a chance to speak again.

My heart dropped a little bit at the sight of Alex standing over the cot, peering down at the baby. I'd been hopeful that he was over admiring him from a distance.

"Pick him up," I ordered.

Alex glanced up at me. "No. He's sleeping. He's fine."

My eyes darted around the room; looking for any excuse I could find to make him lift his son out of the crib. "He needs a bath." I walked over to the baby bath in the corner of the room and wheeled it over to the sink. "You get him ready and I'll fill it."

"Stop it, Charli," mumbled Alex. "There's no problem here. Stop looking for one."

All of my breath escaped me in a frustrated huff. "Fine," I replied stubbornly. "I'll bathe him myself."

Alex stepped aside and motioned toward the baby with his hand. "Up to you."

If there was an award given for mean sister of the year, I was a serious contender. Jack was truly asleep. Disturbing him to give him a bath was unkind, but I did it and he didn't go quietly.

His tiny little cry travelled all the way through me, and when I glanced up at Alex and noticed him chewing his bottom lip, I knew it was affecting him too.

"He doesn't like the water, Charli," he muttered.

I lifted the baby to my shoulder and covered him with a towel. "He's a Blake. How could he not like the water?"

Alex didn't speak again. He didn't need to. Jack was protesting enough for the both of them. As I lowered the tiny boy into the water, his cry amplified. "Jack, please," I begged. "I know I'm a bit out of practice, but you're making me look bad."

He obviously wasn't listening. The heartbreaking little trill continued. After just a minute, Alex had reached his limit. Rather than step in and take over, or demand that I hand him his son, he decided to leave. "I'm going upstairs to see Gabi," he muttered. "I'll be back soon."

He didn't give me a chance to tell him what a coward I thought he was. He practically bolted for the door.

I lifted the clean but wailing baby out of the bath and bundled him up in a towel. "Don't take it personally, Jack," I whispered. "Dad doesn't do crying."

***

Settling the baby was easier than I thought it would be. As soon as he was dressed and comfortable, he quietened down. I spent a long time cradling him in my arms as we wandered around the nursery. I would've ventured further but didn't want to push my luck. According to

Hannah, I was already breaking rules by being in there unsupervised to begin with. Fortunately, I had a good view of the reception area from the doorway.

Micky was the nurse on duty that morning, and she had her work cut out for her trying to discharge the Davis family. Wade stood at the counter, presumably taking care of the paperwork while Jasmine sat on the small sofa surrounded by their army of mini Beautifuls.

I hadn't seen the twins in a long time, and was surprised by how much they'd grown. Cheynie was bouncing around on the cushion beside Jasmine – who seemed oblivious to the fact that her daughter was coming dangerously close to whacking her newborn baby in the head with the kiddy size umbrella she had in her hand. Lincoln was standing to the left of the couch, stripping the leaves off a decorative pot plant.

"Is your name really Micky?" Wade asked, leaning over the counter to get a better look at her nametag.

"Yes." Her dull reply sounded nothing like the upbeat girl I'd met the day before. "It really is."

Wade flashed her his best beefcake grin. "Oh, Micky, you're so fine you blow my mind."

Wade's mind had been blown long before that moment. Perhaps Micky realised it too, which is why she didn't call security and have him ejected from the building. "Like I haven't heard that before." She shoved a stack of papers at him. "Sign these, please."

"Hurry up, babes," demanded Jasmine, bouncing Lachlan far too roughly on her knee. "I've got a nail appointment at eleven."

Slightly appalled and extremely amused, I turned around and headed over to Jack's cot. "You're going to grow up with those monsters," I whispered to him. "I hope you're ready for that."

27. LIMITS

It was a long morning. I was bored, but determined to stay put. I hated that Jack spent so much time alone but on the plus side, it didn't seem to bother him. It brought comfort that he was so quiet. Gabrielle was probably going to need a lot of recovery time, and a placid baby would probably make things easier.

Hannah came on shift at twelve. We chatted for a little bit, mainly about the Lost Boys. "Don't take any nonsense from them, Charli," she warned. "Tyler takes a few too many liberties at times."

"Oh, I don't know." I grinned at her. "Urging me to leave my husband, dump my kid and move back to the Cove seems perfectly reasonable."

Her head lolled back as she slapped her palm against her forehead. "Oh, my God. He really said that?"

"Yeah." I laughed. "He really did."

The phone on the desk beeped and Hannah excused herself to answer it. I checked on Jack, sat back down on the chair and continued reading the not-so fascinating brochure I'd found about breast-feeding techniques.

I didn't get through much of it before Hannah reappeared at the doorway. "You're needed upstairs, Charli."

I'd been quite relaxed until then, but nervousness quickly kicked in. "Is Gabi okay?"

Her rigid nod wasn't very believable. "Everything is fine, but your dad needs you," she replied. "Give me a minute and I'll take you up there."

Hannah disappeared down the corridor, returning a minute later with Nurse Nasty in tow, presumably to hold the fort while she was gone.

I followed Hannah into the elevator and demanded information as soon as the doors closed.

"Nothing has changed," she assured me.

Ordinarily, that would've been good news, but change is what the doctors were hoping for. Gabrielle wasn't responding to treatment.

"They're going to remove her breathing tube and replace it with a tracheal tube," she explained.

"I don't know what that means," I replied, shaking my head.

Hannah had an uncanny knack of explaining things simply and thoroughly in just a few sentences. By the time the doors opened, I knew more about tracheal intubation than I wanted to, and I understood exactly why she was taking me to Alex.

"The doctors have tried to explain the process to him, but he's freaking out a little bit."

I knew why. Of all the medical intervention Gabrielle had endured, seeing the tube down her throat is what hurt Alex the most. Intubating her was going to be far worse. "Of course he is, Hannah," I muttered. "He's just been told that they're going to put a hole in her throat."

We passed through two sets of double doors to get to a tiny room that reminded me of a holding cell in a jail. In fairness, it was probably slightly more welcoming. There was a small sofa, two small chairs and a few crappy generic prints hanging on the light blue walls.

Alex was there too, sitting on the edge of the sofa with his face buried in his hands.

"I'll leave you alone for a minute," murmured Hannah.

When she pulled the door closed, the room got even smaller. I quickly concluded that this was the bad news room. This was where relatives were sent to freak out and grieve in private.

I sat down next to Alex, hooked my arm through his and pressed my face against his upper arm. I didn't dare speak. I just waited for him to say something.

"They're going to cut a hole in her throat," he finally mumbled.

Word for word, his coarse breakdown of the procedure was exactly what I expected. It was all he would've heard while they were explaining it to him.

"She'll be more comfortable," I quietly reasoned. "They're doing it to help her."

Alex shrugged me away and stood up. Moving to the other side of the room was pointless. It was so small that I could have reached out and grabbed him from where I sat.

"They keep telling me they're helping her," he told me. "Why are they putting her through this?"

I had no answers for him and knew better than to pretend otherwise. "You just have to trust that they know what they're doing."

"She's not getting better, Charli." He turned around and rested his head against the wall. "She's dying."

No one had ever told him that. He'd drawn that horrible conclusion on his own because every time he dared to hope, he was knocked down with more bad news.

Everyone has a limit, and Alex had reached his. He let out the most gut-wrenching moan I'd ever heard and slammed his fists into the wall. Then he went silent and still, which was even harder to watch. I made my way over to him and wrapped my arms around his middle.

His head and hands remained pressed up against the wall as if he was trying to push his way out of the room.

I pressed my cheek against his back and held him tightly as silent sobs invaded his body. I closed my eyes, thinking back to the conversations we used to have when I was a kid.

Alex had spent more than his fair share of time standing at the bottom of the big tree in our front yard over the years. He'd try and coax me down, and I'd order him to go away.

"Never going to happen, Charli," he'd say. "You need me to stand here. You just don't realise it."

I had needed him, which is why I was prepared to hold my position indefinitely. He needed me now. He just didn't realise it.

The nightmare we were stuck in was impossibly slow moving. It gave Alex too much thinking time, and it wasn't doing him any good. In a sure-fire sign that he wasn't thinking clearly, he finally broke my hold, turned around and huffed out a few ridiculous instructions. "Tell them no," he ordered, pointing at the door. "Go out there and tell them they're not to touch her."

He sounded so desperate that I found myself nodding in reply. Alex mimicked me, nodding in return as if that somehow sealed the deal.

"I'll talk to them," I promised. "I'll tell them."

It was a big fat lie, but it was necessary. Alex calmed in an instant. I even managed to talk him into going back downstairs to spend time with Jack so when it came to lying to my father, it was one of my more successful efforts.

I walked him to the elevator and then went in search of Hannah. ICU wasn't her territory so not surprisingly; she wasn't at the nurse's station. After quickly explaining the situation to the nurse behind the desk, she kindly picked up the phone and tracked her down.

The next time the elevator door opened, Hannah was in it. The woman was like an angel. Every single time we needed her, she was there.

I wasn't sure where she was leading me as we walked along the corridor. I used the time to fill her in on Alex's dreadful mindset.

"At the end of the day, Charli, nothing has changed," she reasoned, pushing through a set of double doors. "Gabi's condition hasn't deteriorated. We would've hoped to see improvement by now, but she's certainly not worsened."

"Alex doesn't see it that way," I replied. "He's struggling. I need you to tell the doctors to hold off intubating her for a while – just a few hours."

No amount of extra time was likely to change Alex's mind, but at least it would give me a chance to try and calm him down.

Hannah stopped walking, halting both of us. "I can't tell them that, Charli," she said sympathetically.

"I'll tell them," I offered desperately. "Take me to a doctor."

I spent the rest of the long walk down the corridor steeling myself to deal with an uppity old doctor in a white coat – a suitor for Nurse Nasty perhaps. The reality was much different.

Doctor McCane was young and female – probably younger than Gabi. Hannah gave her a quick rundown, but completely omitted my reason for wanting to talk to her.

I prayed I was articulate enough to explain. I'd already decided to call Adam and get him to plead our case if I failed. "Just until morning," I begged. "My dad just needs a bit of time to get his head around it."

Her mouth formed a tight line and I instantly knew I wasn't winning. The woman had iced water running through her veins. "Ms Décarie will be more comfortable once the tracheal tube is in place," she explained. "It will also aid in keeping her lungs clear."

I was shaking my head the whole time she spoke. "She's not Ms Décarie," I said sourly. "Her name is Gabrielle. You don't know anything about her. You don't know anything about us. You don't know that I've just spent the last twenty-four hours desperately trying to hold my father together because he thinks she's dying."

Hannah stepped to the side and grabbed my arm. "Calm down, Charli," she quietly urged.

I jerked my arm free, just as hot tears began trickling down my cheeks. "I will not calm down," I growled. "I know a small delay won't be detrimental to Gabi's treatment." I'd shamelessly stolen that line from Hannah, which is why I managed to say it with the utmost of confidence. "All I am asking for is a few hours. If you deny me, it's only because you're pulling rank."

"You're asking me to delay treatment." There was a hint of condescension to her tone now, which made my reply extra sour.

"No, I'm asking you to set your God complex aside for a minute and show some compassion."

After a long moment of deliberation, Doctor McCane grew a heart and yielded. "I'll reschedule the procedure for first thing in the morning. I'm not prepared to delay it any further."

I swept my hands through my hair, trying to pull myself together. "Thank you," I breathed. "I'm just asking for a few hours."

The nod she gave was aimed squarely at Hannah, and she didn't look pleased.

I studied Doctor McCane closely as she walked away. She went about her business as if the last few minutes of conversation had never happened.

I, on the other hand, felt as if I'd just gone ten rounds in a boxing ring.

"Nice work," praised Hannah once she was out of earshot. "I'm amazed that went your way. Doctors usually don't like being called out on their God complexes."

I looked across at her, immediately noticing her sly smile.

"I'm used to it," I muttered. "My brother-in-law thinks he's God too."

She let out a quiet chuckle. "Do you want to visit Gabrielle before you go?"

"No." I didn't even need to think about it.

I'd been unwittingly forced into the position of taking charge. Historically, that had been Alex's job. I'd always believed that he could fix the whole world when I needed him to, but my eyes had been opened in the most brutal of ways. He wasn't quite that powerful.

I declined Hannah's offer of visiting Gabi before leaving ICU because I was scared. That meant I wasn't powerful either.

Hannah didn't push the issue, because Hannah doesn't push. Instead, she escorted me back to the maternity ward to continue the mammoth task of trying to hold my family together.

***

I spent a long time spying on Alex and Jack through the viewing window, which was pointless. Nothing ever changed. My dad sat beside him, gripping the edge of his cot. He'd occasionally pat his back or fuss with his blankets but gave the poor kid nothing else.

Just pick him up, I silently willed a hundred times.

He didn't. And the sad, disconnected moment they were stuck in continued.

28. WALKING AWAY

It was becoming harder and harder to talk to Alex. The late afternoon drive back to the Cove was a repeat of the day before; only this time the long lulls in conversation didn't bother me.

I wasn't in the mood for small talk any more than he was, but I still felt compelled to try. "I got an email from Adam earlier," I said dully. "He called Monique and Richard."

Alex took his eyes off the road the glare at me. "Why?"

"Because Gabi's parents need to know," I replied. "I assume you'd want to know if I was in ICU."

From the corner of my eye I could see his knuckles whiten as he tightened his grip on the steering wheel. "I was going to call them."

We both knew that was a lie. He couldn't get his act together enough to hold his baby son. Calling Gabrielle's parents was not high on his agenda.

"They're holidaying in Cape Verde," I added. "They're getting the first flight out but they won't be here until the end of the week."

The car slowed as he glanced across to growl at me. "Why are they coming here? I don't want them here."

"They're her parents, Alex." I raised my voice to match his. "They need to be here."

"I don't want them here," he yelled. "I don't want anyone here."

I assumed that by everyone, he meant me too. Too hurt to reply, I rested my head against the cold window, purely so he wouldn't see me cry. I didn't bother speaking again for the rest of the journey. If that upset him, it certainly didn't show. When we got home, he slammed the car door and stormed up to the house before I'd even undone my seatbelt.

Alex felt crowded, and yet I'd never felt more alone in all my life.

It was confusing and unfair.

I got out of the car and spent the next minute or two wandering around the yard. I was underdressed for the cold dusk air, but it was still preferable to going inside.

My father didn't agree. He appeared on the porch a minute later and ordered me inside. "It's cold."

"I know it's bloody cold," I yelled. "I don't care."

"Why are you staying out here?"

"Because I don't want to deal with you," I shouted. "Just leave me alone for a minute."

"I don't think I can do that, Charli."

"Well, try." I threw my arms out wide before slapping them down on my sides. "I don't feel like being your emotional punching bag any more. I've had enough for one day."

Alex stared down at me for an uncomfortably long time. I stood my ground by staring right back.

"I'm sorry," he said finally.

"You need to sort yourself out," I demanded, pointing at him. "Stop reading so far ahead. You've lost nothing, Alex." Frustration drove my voice louder. I was practically screaming now. "Everything you love is still here. Gabi's here. Jack's here, and for some crazy reason, I'm here too."

I wasn't overly surprised when he turned around and walked back into the house. Alex didn't deal with crazy. Alex wasn't dealing with anything lately. That's why his son had spent the majority of his short life cooped up alone in the hospital nursery.

In a move reminiscent of the petulant child I used to be, I stomped my way over to the lemon tree; picked the biggest one I saw and pegged it at the house. Surprisingly, lemons make a hell of a thud when they smash against a screen door.

My ten-year-old self would've bolted after that, but my twenty-four-year-old self stood firm and bravely waited for the fallout.

Alex didn't look too pissed when he came back out a few seconds later. If anything, he looked confused. "What was that?" After a quick glance around, he spotted the offending fruit on the porch. "You threw a lemon at my house?"

"You walked away!" I screamed. "I'm so sick of you walking away!"

Now he looked pissed. "I went inside to get you a coat." He held it out to prove it and then stepped off the veranda.

I started to cry as he walked toward me, and it wasn't pretty. It was the hard, ugly sobbing that only comes when you've no idea what else to do.

"And just so we're clear, Charlotte," he thrust the coat at me, "I have never, ever walked away from you. Not once in your whole life."

"I'm not talking about me," I sobbed into my hands.

The gentle gesture of draping the coat around my shoulders didn't match his angry tone. "Who then? Jack?"

"All you have to do is love him. It's not that difficult."

Alex grabbed my hands and prised them from my face. "I love both of my children." He said it through gritted teeth, shaking me so hard by the wrists that I stumbled forward.

For the very first time in my life, I was frightened of him, and something in my expression let him know. He released me in an instant.

The short but nasty exchange left Alex far more wounded than me. He was shaking, and the terrible look on his face was one of pure self-loathing.

I could overlook the anger because it wasn't what was driving him. He was scared, and had been for days. "What are you most afraid of?" I asked quietly.

"That Gabi – "

"I'm not talking about Gabi," I interrupted. "I'm talking about Jack."

He blew out a long breath and looked to the darkening sky above. "I can't connect with him, Charli. We missed a step."

"What step?"

"The beginning," he said sadly. "I don't know how to get it back."

Adam once told me of a moment he shared with Bridget just after she was born. I'd never forgotten it. Perhaps – like a treasured wish – I'd been saving it for this moment.

She looked up at me, and I knew she was looking further than my eyes. It was a look reserved just for me. Bridget knew I was her dad, and she knew how much I love her mother.

I was wrong when I told Alex he hadn't lost anything. If that was the moment he felt he'd missed out on he had every right to feel bereft.

"It's not too late," I assured. "Just start again."

Alex folded his arms tightly across his chest, probably to stop his heart from falling out and hitting the dirt. "I don't think he even knows I'm his father."

I shook my head, and quickly swiped a rogue tear from my cheek. "It won't matter. He already loves you." I spoke with absolute certainty because I knew I was telling the truth. "You're my dad too, Alex. I loved you for seventeen years before finding that out."

I'd been trying to hit on the right combination of words to say since I arrived. Those were it. I could almost see the despair lift from his shoulders.

"I've been looking for magic," he confessed, mumbling down at the ground. "Anything to help us through this."

I was the only person on earth who he would've admitted that to. For that reason alone, I didn't make a big deal of it. "I can point you in the direction of magic," I offered. "Where is my box of wishes buried?"

Alex lifted his head and gazed across the yard. "A box of trinkets won't fix us, Charli." He spoke gently, as if he felt sorry for me.

I roughly grabbed his sleeve and turned him to face me. "You reburied that box, not me," I sternly reminded. "You believed in it. Don't start second-guessing now. What do you have to lose?"

He slowly shook his head. "Nothing," he conceded.

"Great." I huffed out the word in a sharp breath. "So let's dig it up."

***

Daylight was all but gone by the time we unearthed the box. If we were hanging out in a cemetery digging up a coffin, the cold dark night would've been the perfect backdrop. But we weren't. We were standing between a couple of geranium bushes freezing our butts off while we dug up a secret cache of toys and shells.

As soon as I picked it up, I tore the plastic wrapping off and held it out to my father.

Alex dropped the shovel and took it from my grasp. "What am I supposed to do with it?"

I didn't know. Even I could admit that the notion of a box of wishes was slightly off kilter. I'd spent a lifetime saving them. Spending them wasn't my forte. "Give them to Jack," I decided. "Every last one of them."

***

Alex didn't dally. I got the impression he was keen to offload the box, probably fearing that if he held on to it for too long, crazy would really take hold.

"I'm going back to the hospital," he told me.

"Tonight?" I asked incredulously.

We'd been home for less than an hour, after driving for an hour to get here.

"Yeah," he said softly. "I'll give the box to Jack and then go and see Gabs. I want to have a chat with her."

I nodded, unwilling to press him for any more information.

Recharging only slightly, Alex showered and grabbed a quick bite to eat before heading for the door. "Please stay here tonight," he said, grabbing his keys off the table.

I glanced through to the lounge room. "On the couch?"

Alex smiled at me. "It's a nice couch."

I pulled a face letting him know it was less than ideal. "Yeah, okay."

Just as he got to the door, he turned back to face me. "I'll make it up to you, Charli," he promised.

"Make what up?"

"Everything," he replied simply.

Alex

29. SEA LEGS

Arriving at the hospital at night threw me straight back to the midnight arrival we'd made just four days ago. There were some differences. I wasn't excited this time, and Gabi wasn't by my side. I was travelling solo tonight, and carrying a broken wooden box of wishes under my arm.

I couldn't explain why. I could only put it down to the fact that I was desperate enough to try anything to get my little world back on track.

The maternity ward took on a whole new feel after dark. The lights were low and it was deathly quiet. I made my way over to the nurse's station, hoping to find some sign of life.

I recognised the nurse behind the desk immediately. "You were there the day my son was born," I remembered, setting the box down on the high counter. "You wheeled his cot into the room."

I'd only caught a fleeting glance at her as she rushed past me, but she was memorable because her hair was the same coppery colour as Gabrielle's.

"I did," she replied, extending her hand over the high counter. "I'm Hilary."

"Alex," I replied, shaking her hand.

She had a great smile. I'd missed that detail the first time I met her. There hadn't been a whole lot of smiling going on that day.

"What's in the box?" she asked, pointing at it.

I was just about to answer her when a little cry rang out of from a few feet away in the nursery. Straight away, I knew it was Jack. There was no other sound like it.

"He's calling for you," said Hilary. She glanced up at the clock on the wall. "He shouldn't be hungry yet. He probably just needs a cuddle."

"He needs his mother." The words fell out of my mouth before I could stop them.

Hilary overlooked my harsh tone, and the pain behind the words. "You'll do for now," she quipped.

My efforts at comforting him had been appalling so far, but she didn't need to know that. I forced a smile, picked up my box and headed into the nursery.

Jack seemed resigned to the fact that I wasn't good for anything more than a few pats on the back and subpar conversation. I settled him quickly, rearranged his blankets and sat down beside him.

"Your sister wanted me to give you this." I held the broken box up so he'd get a better look at it. "It's full of wishes. You have a nice stash here."

Jack was wide awake. It gave me hope that he was listening to me.

"How about a bit of show and tell?" I suggested. I picked a white plastic horse out of the box. "This one's special," I explained. "Apparently he's worth a wish because his tail is black."

Jack's perfectly timed little groan made me chuckle. "I know, mate. But who are we to argue? Your sister likes to make her own rules."

Besides the storm shells, I didn't recognise anything else in the box. I doubt Charli would've either. With the exception of a few weeks after Bridget was born, the box had been buried for nearly two decades.

A green plastic dice came next. "No idea where she got this from – a Christmas cracker, maybe." I carefully set it down on the edge of his cot and dug my hand back into the box.

I was so unprepared for the next find that my hand shook as I picked it up. "A purple turtle," I announced, setting it down next to the dice. "This one might actually be a genuine bit of magic, Jack."

I spent an abnormal amount of time staring at it while I searched for logical explanation.

As a child, Charli had been a hoarder when it came to wishes. It wasn't too shocking to discover that she'd collected a tiny ceramic purple turtle along the way. What I couldn't put down to coincidence was that it had a pink flower painted on its back, just like the one on Gabrielle's mural.

Thanks to years I'd spent fuelling my daughter's imagination, I'd fumbled my way through life looking for acts of magic. My faith in the entire concept had crumbled over the past few days simply because I hadn't been able to find any – until now.

"We're back in the game, baby," I whispered to my son.

The reason why was clear, and not overly complicated.

Gabrielle's theory behind changing the colour of the crows and turtle flooded my mind with such force that I said the words out loud. "The things that scare us are never as daunting if you change the way you look at them."

Finding magic is one thing. Acting on it is another. If you do nothing, the moment is lost. If you take the time to work out the deeper meaning, you carry the moment with you forever.

I was determined not to lose it so despite the fact that my hands were trembling, I leaned down and picked my child up for the very first time. He was soft and warm and fit perfectly in the crook of my elbow. I sat back down on the chair and cradled him against my chest. "We'll sit for a minute," I told him. "Just until I get my sea legs."

The problem with fear is that it's generally all consuming. The biggest worry I had was that eventually I'd lose the ability to feel anything else. The thought of losing Gabrielle scared me. The prospect of raising Jack alone scared me. Everything about Jack scared me. I had to get past it, for all of our sakes.

The baby didn't seem to mind my unsteadiness. His blue eyes were wide and looking straight at me. I met his gaze, and in a move that was long overdue, I changed the way I looked at him.

"I won't make you any more promises," I said.

I was worried that I'd been lying to him this whole time. For days, I'd been telling him that things were going to get better. Nothing was better. We were still in limbo and I had no idea how long it would last, or what the outcome would be.

"I'm not sure if things are going to work out or not, Jack, but I do know that we're going to be okay." I dipped my head and pressed my lips against his warm head. "I'll make sure of it."

I had a lot of ground to make up to both of my children. I decided to get back to basics and start making amends the best way I knew how.

Feeling much steadier on my feet, I carried Jack over to the sink. "Baby baths are overrated," I declared, pushing the plug into place. "How are you supposed to get a feel for swimming if you've no room to move?"

Jack seemed to know what was coming. He wriggled in my arms so I changed my hold on him and raised him to my shoulder.

When the sink was nearly full, I turned off the taps, lowered my baby onto the counter and undressed him. Predictably, he let me know what a dumb idea he thought it was. I lifted him up, cuddling the naked bundle against my chest as he did his pissed off kitten routine.

I worked hard to reassure him. "Midnight swims are sublime." I flicked my free hand through the water, double-checking the temperature. "The water's warm, the company is decent and you have the whole sink to yourself."

Being bathed was Jack's very first pet hate. My plan was to convince him that that was because he'd been doing it wrong. With my hand wrapped firmly around his chest, I lowered the tiny boy into the water belly first and slowly swiped him forward through the water.

Within seconds, the wailing dulled to intermittent little groans. "See?" I crooned. "It's all in the technique."

A stainless steel sink was no comparison to the ocean, but Jack seemed to get the gist. He was barely making a sound now, but his little legs were slow dancing under the water.

"Unlike your mother, I don't know about languages or art, but I do know about water. It's infinite and deep and powerful, which is why you should never turn your back on it," I explained. "It's also humbling and calming and healing."

I felt an invisible whack right between my shoulder blades as I heard my own words. I'd just described far more than the ocean. I'd completely summed up fatherhood.

***

I stayed with the baby long enough to give him his next feed and settle him back to sleep. The shift between us was incredible. In spite of everything, I'd found a way of connecting with him.

Charli was right. There was joy to be found, and realising it somehow made dealing with everything else easier.

30. LETTING GO

No matter what time of the day or night I visited ICU, the atmosphere was always the same. It was bleak, unwelcoming and clinical, even at midnight.

Gabrielle's appearance no longer shocked me, and I'd given up expecting her to look better. Her right hand was one of the few parts of her body that was untouched and undamaged by needles or tape. I constantly held it when I sat with her because it was the closest reminder I had of a time when things were different.

I spent the first few minutes telling her all about Jack's real first bath. "He took to it like a little duck – a little Blake duck." I hummed the words against her hand. "But he protested at first like a little Décarie."

Silence is a scary sound, and I'd heard a lot of it lately. Even the constant beeping of machines didn't hide the lack of conversation. I kept talking to her because I had to believe she could hear me. If I lost that hope, I'd have nothing.

"I want you to know something, Gabs," I whispered. I watched her chest rise and fall three times before speaking again. It took me that long to find words. "If you've had enough, I understand."

Doctors and specialists had been coming up with plan after plan of making her well for days. It made no sense that she wasn't improving. The tiniest part of my heart wondered if she was just trying to let go. And if that was the case, she needed to know that we'd be alright.

"I wouldn't want you to worry about us." I swallowed hard; trying to hold back the inevitable sob that was caught in my throat. "Because I'd find a way to make us okay."

My chest felt entirely too heavy. I wasn't giving her permission to leave us. I'd spent hour after hour begging her to fight harder and get well, but she wasn't, and I had to concede that maybe she wasn't going to.

I readjusted my hold on her hand, savouring her touch. If Gabrielle had the slightest level of awareness, she would've understood why. Her hand was a perfect fit for mine, and I held it every chance I got, even as we slept.

"I'll still hold your hand at night." I choked out the whispered promise. "Even if you're gone."

It was the most private conversation I'd ever had in my life, and I wasn't expecting to be interrupted. The knock on the open door startled me so much that I jumped.

"Sorry," apologised Hilary. "Didn't mean to scare you."

I rubbed my hands against my eyes and blew out a steadying breath. "You didn't. Is Jack alright?"

"He's perfect." Hilary stepped to the side and wheeled the little plastic box she'd been hiding from view into the room. "I just thought he'd like to hang out with his mum for a bit."

It was the kindest, most compassionate gesture imaginable, and I wanted to kiss her for making it happen. I managed to hold off by picking my son up instead. "Are you breaking the rules by doing this?" I asked.

"It's my fourth nightshift in a row." Hilary winked at me. "I make my own rules now."

I smiled gratefully. "Thank you."

"No worries," she replied. "I'll wait at the nurse's station. I heard a rumour that they're stockpiling biscuits up here. If you need me, just yell."

"I will."

"But not too loudly," she teased, backing away. "Those ICU girls have no sense of humour."

***

I wasted no time in reuniting Gabi with her baby. As soon as the awesome renegade nurse left, I gently lowered Jack into his mother's sleeping arms. I kept a protective hand on him in case he wriggled, but Jack didn't move. It was as if he knew he needed to be still for her.

Predictably Gabi didn't move either, but something in my soul told me she knew he was there.

I was quiet for a minute because I hated the thought of Gabrielle hearing the tremor in my voice when I spoke; especially considering the moment was essentially good. When I thought I'd pulled myself together enough, I let her know how perfect they looked together. "It's all up to you now, babe," I whispered.

31. READING AHEAD

Despite the late night spent at the hospital, I woke before dawn the next morning feeling anxious and slightly ill because of it. The first thing I did was check my phone for missed calls, because that's what I did whenever I was away from Gabrielle. The second thing I did was breathe a sigh of relief because there weren't any. I always did that too.

Getting back to sleep would be impossible so I didn't try. I got up instead, and put my plan of reconnecting with my oldest child into action.

Salt water cures everything. My beliefs had taken a beating lately, but I was certain that one was absolute fact. Once I'd loaded our boards and gear into the car, I headed back inside and woke Charli.

"It's not even light yet," she complained.

"I know," I replied, tossing a coat at her. "Hurry up. The day is wasting."

***

Charli's strong affinity to nature and the ocean was predestined. A child who grows up seeing nature's beauty and power on a daily basis is bound to look at things differently.

Mother nature was at her best in Pipers Cove – and most days she was pissed. As a rule, the ocean was wild, the coastline was jagged and the surf was amazing because of it.

Charli stopped whining about being woken the second her feet hit the sand. There was a slight offshore wind, which meant the waves that were rolling in were well formed and breaking cleanly. The conditions were perfect, and Charli knew it.

"What do you think?" I asked, glancing across at her.

"I think I'm home," she replied wistfully. "What do you think?"

I shifted my focus from the waves to the sky above. It didn't look like a winter sky. The sun was rising fast, casting an orange glow through the streaky cirrus clouds.

"I think today will be different," I told her. I wasn't prepared to say it would be better, but I knew it would be different.

Plenty had changed overnight. Bonding with Jack and reuniting him with his mum had been a turning point. I vowed not to take any more on board than I had to, and felt remarkably stronger because of it.

"I think so too." Charli turned her head, flashing me an errant smile. "Today is the day I'm going to beat you out to the break." She backed up the cocky statement by bolting for the surf.

I watched as she dropped her board down and launched herself onto it. After dragging her arms through the water in a few long strokes, she paused to study the surf.

She was searching for a channel – a break in the white-water where the resistance was low to make paddling out to the break easier. It was as close as Charli ever gets to looking before she leaps. It was insightful and awesome – and I'd taught her to do it.

She sat up on her board and turned around when I called out her name.

"What?" she asked, raising her voice to reach me.

I folded my arms and rocked back on my heels, sinking my feet into the cold sand. "Look how well you turned out," I gloated.

The fifty metres of water between us did nothing to dull her smile, or her voice. "Yeah, good job, Dad," she called. "I'm nearly normal."

***

Charli had spent six months out of the water. I'd only been out for a week, but it felt like six months. Perhaps that's why neither of us saw a problem with whittling away three hours in the surf.

The ocean was our place, and it had always been that way. We didn't say a lot, because we didn't need to. Just spending time out there together was enough.

It was just after eleven when we finally made our way to shore. Charli handed me my phone that she'd wrapped up in her towel.

"I've missed a few calls from the hospital," I muttered, staring at the screen.

"Call them back," urged Charli, mussing her hair with the towel.

My heart began to thump a little harder. "No." I switched off my phone. "We'll be there soon anyway."

She nodded, whether she approved or not. "Okay," she said quietly. "Let's go."

We were almost at the base of the trail before I spoke again. "I told Gabi she should let go if she wants to." I blurted it out quickly, desperate to be rid of the words. "Maybe she's gone."

Charli slowly turned to face me, looking nowhere near as appalled as I thought she would. "You're reading ahead again, Dad. Don't do it," she warned.

She was right – again. Just one seed of doubt had the power to knock me straight back to the ugly mindset I'd worked so hard to shake off, and getting past it wasn't easy. "They're putting that tube thing in her throat this morning," I reminded. "What if – "

"Stop." She put her hand up as if I needed visual instruction. "Tell me something true."

I frowned, having no clue what she meant. "I don't – "

"You're giving me lots of what-ifs. Give me a truth. Tell me anything you like, as long as it's true." Charli smiled as if we didn't have a care in the world, and at that moment, we didn't.

"I like it when you call me Dad," I offered. "Even if it's accidental."

She shook her head, but the smile remained. "It's never accidental."

"Really?"

"Never," she insisted, shifting her board to her other arm. "Sometimes I say it because I think you need to hear it. And sometimes it's just because I need to say it."

Whatever I'd taught my daughter over the years would forever pale in comparison to the things I'd learned from her.

I hadn't made Charli. She'd made me.

32. AWARENESS

I was hopeful that Hannah would be there when we arrived at the hospital. We'd done some serious bonding in the past few days, mainly over vomit and bad news, but it still counted.

I wasn't so lucky.

The second Charli and I stepped out of the elevator; a tiny nurse in chunky white shoes came charging at us.

"Brace yourself, Alex," muttered Charli from the corner of her mouth. "Here comes Nurse Nasty."

"Mr Blake," she called, waving a stack of papers at me. "You need to go upstairs this minute."

I didn't ask her why because I didn't want to know. Nothing about her demeanour led me to think it was for anything good.

"I'll wait with Jack," offered Charli.

I nodded, but must've looked pitiful.

My daughter reached out, grabbed my arm and pulled me away from the pushy nurse. "Do you want me to come with you?"

"No," I replied, trying to sound sure. "Whatever will be, will be, right?"

Nurse Nasty wedged her foot in the way of the closing elevator door. "Now, Mr Blake," she ordered.

***

Hannah's colleague wasn't chatty. We stood side by side in the elevator, staring at the doors as if they were about to slide open at any second. I knew better. The ride up to ICU always seemed to take forever.

"Not much of a talker, are you?" I asked, folding my arms. "What's your name?"

The nurse kept her focus firmly on the doors. "Pamela Lilley."

I lazily turned my head in her direction. "Well, Pamela Lilley, you have a lovely name."

She barely cast a glance in my direction, making it perfectly clear that she wasn't the least bit charmed by me.

"Most people associate lilies with death," I continued. "They're funeral flowers, right?"

"I believe so," she muttered.

"They're not, you know. They represent chastity and virtue." I tilted my head to the side and spoke softly, as if I was letting her in on some big secret. "They also symbolised the Virgin Mary's role as Queen of the Angels, so Lilley is the perfect name for a nurse, don't you think?"

The woman formerly known as Nurse Nasty turned to face me. She'd thawed a little bit, and it was spectacular. "How do you know that?"

I shrugged. "My kid told me." The elevator doors opened and I stepped out before turning back to Pamela. "She knows all the important stuff."

If Pamela planned to accompany me to the ward, she was too slow. The doors closed and the tiny, stunned nurse disappeared from view.

I was almost smiling when I turned around. And then I remembered where I was.

I never got used to being in ICU, nor did I want to. I headed toward the nurse's station, searching for anyone who was prepared to deal with me.

No one was there.

Ordinarily, I would've continued on to Gabi's room, but this day wasn't ordinary. I'd missed eight calls that morning. Something had changed, and I was scared to find out what it was.

I stood by the desk like a lost kid for a full five minutes before someone put me out of my misery. The elevator doors slid open and Hannah rushed out.

"Hey," she blurted. "You waited for me?"

I half nodded, pretending to know what she meant.

Hannah grabbed my arm and started leading me toward Gabrielle's room. "I got here as quickly as I could," she told me. "It's mayhem this morning. Both delivery suites are busy."

"Why are you up here then?" I asked quietly.

Hannah stopped walking, pulling me to a stop. "You don't even know, do you?" I shook my head and Hannah's grip on my arm got tighter. "Gabi's awake, Alex. She came on in leaps and bounds during the night. They woke her up just after seven this morning."

It had been so long since I'd heard anything good that my mind seemed to reject the news. I stared blankly at her, trying to work through it. "That's why they called me?" I asked finally.

"Well, yeah." Hannah laughed. "We thought you'd want to know."

Things slowly became clearer as relief flooded my heart, drowning out the crippling sadness that had weighed on me for days.

I really didn't know Hannah that well so there was a fair chance that throwing my arms around her and hugging her half to death was inappropriate, but I did it anyway.

"Okay, okay," she gasped, pushing on my chest. "Enough now."

I took a big step back and held up both hands to prove I posed no further danger. "I'm sorry." I grinned as I said it, which proved only that I wasn't sorry at all. I was elated and hopeful and thankful.

Hannah talked as she walked. It was her thing. "She's going to be really groggy for a while. Don't expect too much riveting conversation."

I don't know what she said after that. The minute we got to the door of Gabrielle's room, everything stopped.

I saw her eyes before anything else. I'd spent days fearing I'd never see them again. For that reason alone, they were the brightest, loveliest shade of green imaginable.

The urge to rush over and take her in my arms didn't kick in as quickly as I expected it to. I was having trouble stepping past the doorway.

It wasn't until Hannah pushed past me and made her way across to Gabi's bed that my mind gave in and finally accepted that what I was seeing was true.

She was awake. She looked frail and sick, but she was awake.

"You had us a bit worried, Gabrielle," Hannah joked, pushing something at the back of the bed. The headboard lifted, raising Gabi almost to a sitting position, and Hannah's work was done. She passed me at the doorway, smiling brightly. "I'll leave you two kids alone."

It was the moment I'd longed for, but reacting to it took time. By the time I finally found my feet and made my way over to her, my whole body was shaking. Sitting beside her was a position I'd held for countless hours over the past five days, but this time was different.

Gabrielle was finally with me.

Many of the dreadful wires and leads were gone, and overlooking the ones that remained was easy. To me, she looked perfect.

I took her hand in mine and kissed her fingers, throwing more meaning behind it than I ever had. It was almost odd to feel her squeeze my hand. It was languid and weak, but the power wasn't in her touch. It was in her presence.

Gabi slowly turned her head toward me. "I dreamed he was here with me, Alex." Her voice was gravelly, small – and quite possibly the sweetest sound I'd ever heard.

I reached and tucked her limp hair behind her ear. "Who, Gabs?"

"Baby."

The emotion I felt at that point was like nothing I'd ever experienced in all my life. She remembered Jack being there the night before, which meant she'd at least had some awareness.

I'd been talking to her for days, and she'd heard me.

"He *was* here last night," I confirmed in a quaky voice. "You held him."

A perfect slow smile crept across her face. "I remember."

"I love you, Gabs," I whispered, almost desperately.

"I know," she mumbled. "I remember."

***

Having Gabrielle back changed the way time moved. We didn't do a lot of talking, but I didn't feel the need to make noise and time passed quickly.

Gabi slept in short bursts. Each time she woke, she seemed a little bit more lucid. "I like Jack's name," she said out of the blue.

"You do?" I was surprised for a few reasons. First, she knew his name. And second, she liked it.

"Jacques-Louis David was a French painter," she hoarsely mumbled. "Neoclassical style."

Even in her hazy state, Gabi saw through the tight smile I gave her. She slowly reached out and put her hand on my cheek. "But we shall call him Jack," she whispered.

***

By late afternoon, Gabrielle's mind was completely one-track. Her focus was entirely on seeing our baby son. It was the biggest indication I had that she was on the mend. When Hannah finally wheeled his crib into the room, I thought

Gabi was going to leap out of bed and snatch him up.

I moved quickly to make sure she didn't try. I lifted him out of the cot and raised him to my shoulder, thanking Hannah as she slipped out of the room. I turned back to Gabi, taking a few seconds to etch her expression of sheer wonderment into my soul.

Gabrielle hadn't waited five days for this moment. She'd been waiting for five years.

I walked back to the bed and lowered her most longed for wish into her arms. There was no need to keep a protective hand on Jack this time round. His mother's hold on him would never waver again.

I sat in silence for a long time, watching as they got to know each other. Gabi studied him from head to toe – intently as if she was making up for lost time. Jack was the most placid of babies. Perhaps that's why he didn't complain.

"So much hair," marvelled Gabi, brushing her hand over the top of his head. "Did Charli have a lot of hair?"

"No," I replied smiling. "She was bald until she was one – and bald again at three." Gabrielle frowned, forcing me to elaborate. "Chewing gum." I shook my head. "Terrible ordeal."

She laughed, almost managing to sound like herself. The mere sound made me feel like I'd found something precious again. I reacted to it the only way I possibly could. I carefully leaned across our son and pressed my lips against hers.

It was hard not to reflect on the trauma my family had endured but I'd given up searching for answers. Love doesn't question how or why. It just exists – giving us purpose to get up and fight another day.

Losing the anger and being grateful for the good was important. It was about understanding the difference between darkness and blackness.

For a scary moment, there was an absence of light, which I'd perceived as blackness. Seeing my son in the arms of his mother proved how wrong I'd been. Blackness hadn't clouded or dulled any of us. Darkness finally lifted and we were shining again, just as clearly and brightly as we always had.

33. PRISONER OF WAR

Gabrielle went from strength to strength over the next few days, and slowly but surely life seemed to regain some semblance of normality.

Charli was understandably keen to get back to New York and I urged her to go. Bridget's fourth birthday was just days away, and if she missed it, I'd never forgive myself. I'd kept her to myself for too long.

The plan for that day was to drive her to the airport and spend the rest of the afternoon hanging out with Gabi and Jack at the hospital. It was the last day I'd have them to myself for a while. Gabrielle's parents were due to arrive the next day. Sharing was going to be difficult, but I vowed to try.

I arrived at the cottage much earlier than necessary, which turned out to be a good move.

My daughter was in need of rescuing.

I got out of the car and walked over to the shed. "Should I ask what you're doing up there?" I put my hand to my forehead, shielding my eyes from the sun as I looked up at her.

Charli was sitting on the roof of the shed, leisurely swinging her legs over the edge. "I'm a prisoner of war," she announced.

"The Lost Boys?"

She grinned down at me. "Yeah. They caught wind of the news that I'm going home today."

The fact that they'd taken her prisoner didn't shock me. What surprised me was that they'd managed to get her on to the roof in the first place. "You're off your game, Charlotte." I almost sounded disappointed.

"No," she replied, laughing. "They lifted theirs."

I listened intently as she explained how the Lost Boys had gotten the better of her. She'd caught Mason half way up a ladder, trying to retrieve a lost Frisbee off the shed roof. She'd gallantly moved him aside and climbed up to get it herself.

"The little scammer was crying and everything." She frowned, probably cursing herself for being so gullible. "Before I knew what was happening, Tyler and Sean swooped in and took off with the ladder. They said they'd come back for me when they were sure my plane had taken off."

It was hard not to be impressed by their tenacity. I should probably have been a little alarmed by their tactics as well, but I wasn't. I had trouble letting her go too. "Didn't you think to yell for help?" I asked, doing nothing to hide my wry smile. "Hannah or Flynn would've rescued you."

She turned her head, glancing back at the house next door. "Well, I was going to but then something terrible happened." Her dramatic tone wasn't the least bit believable. "Wade, Jasmine and the non-rhyming juniors turned up next door. I decided to just bunker down and wait for you."

I laughed, mainly at her choice of words. "Gabi worked it out, you know," I said irrelevantly. "The rhyming thing."

"She did?" Her whole face lit up. "Tell me."

Gabrielle was an extremely lateral thinker. She always approached things creatively and indirectly. Perhaps it was because she was an artist. Or maybe it was just because she was brilliant.

Wade wasn't brilliant. He was an idiot who got his words mixed up.

"Lincoln, Lachlan and Cheyne," I announced, looking up at her. "Get it now?"

Charli frowned, gazing out at the ocean in the distance while she pondered my words. "Link, lock and chain," she said finally. "That's almost clever."

I dropped my head, laughing down at the ground. "Almost."

"Go over there and tell them how clever they are," she joked. "And while you're at it, tell the Lost Boys I want my ladder back."

I lifted my head to look at her. "I'm not sure I want to," I admitted. "I like having you around too."

Charli smiled, but it was sad. "I miss my kid – and her father."

There was no better reason to let her go.

"You should get off the roof then," I teased. "You're going to miss your plane."

In a move that made me nervous, she leaned forward, looking down at the ground. "I need a ladder."

"Just jump," I replied.

The smile she flashed me was different this time. It was cheeky and lovely and threw me right back to when she was little. "Will you catch me?" she asked.

I barely hesitated. "Every single time you jump, Charli, I will catch you."

We'd had a lot of very important conversations over the past few days, and this one was shaping up to be no different. Charli knew it too.

"I never doubted it," she replied.

I couldn't quite believe her. Charli had seen me in a completely different light over the past week, and there had been more than one moment that I wasn't necessarily proud of.

"You were my first, Charli," I told her. "No matter what, don't ever forget that."

"First what?"

I shrugged, feeling slightly coy when it came to elaborating. "First love, first child, first always and first forever."

She stood up, steadying herself by stretching out her arms. "Don't make me cry again, Dad," she said in a wobbly voice. "Just get me down from here."

I grabbed my keys from my pocket, unlocked the shed and grabbed a ladder.

When she was safely on ground, I added the last piece to my declaration by pulling her into my arms. "We're a team, Charli," I told her. "The team is just a little bigger now."

"I like it bigger."

"Me too."

I no longer measured the mark I was leaving on the world. I realised that the mark the world left on me was much more important.

Gabrielle's hand fit perfectly in mine. Jack's little body was the perfect fit for the crook of my elbow. And Charli's head fit perfectly under my chin when I hugged her. Those are the marks of a man who has everything.

THE END